Wrong Side of Time

Carrie Hatchett, Space Adventurer Book 4

J.J. GREEN

ISBN: 978-1-913476-16-8

Cover Design by

Illuminated Images & Dark Moon Graphics

CONTENTS

CHAPTER ONE – UNDER ATTACK

Carrie Hatchett fired at the alien running towards her. Two sets of glowing pulses flew out from the lasers she held in either hand, converging on the galloping, green, warty mass of the alien. As the lasers hit, the alien exploded, scattering into wet fragments dripping with blue blood that splattered the walls, floor and ceiling of the starship control centre.

Another alien popped up from behind the navigation desk, its scaly head weaving and ruby eyes flashing. Carrie swung round to fire, but Dave was on it. He blew off the alien's head at the neck before the rest of the body had time to emerge, leaving a smoking stump. He turned to Carrie and flashed a smile. But neither could rest for long. Writhing tentacles were dropping from vents in the ceiling. They squirmed so fast, they were difficult to aim at. Carrie's shots flew wide of the wriggling appendages, nicking the edges. Purple mucus dripped to the floor, but the wounds seemed to have no effect on the beast. More tentacles appeared. Where was its head? Was this alien all tentacles?

Dave had more success. He had managed to sever a few of the limbs completely, and they lay on the floor twisting and twitching, apparently still alive. The tentacles inched slowly towards them across the gore-drenched floor.

"Watch out," exclaimed Dave. "And look—over there in the corner."

Carrie had thought it was just a shadow, but it was thickening and solidifying. Legs grew and a head appeared. No, three heads. On each, a mass of eyes blinked open, deadly pale. Meanwhile, the writhing tentacles on the floor moved closer. For a moment Carrie was distracted from the spectacle of the awful black alien. She blasted the nearest tentacle to fragments. That seemed to kill it. She sent laser pulses into the new tentacles wriggling out of the ceiling vents.

A glint of silver in the corner drew Carrie's eyes back to the black alien. It had arms now. At least five or six, and each held a weapon.

"We're done for," Carrie said. "We'll never kill that thing."

"Speak for yourself," said Dave, sending rapid bolts of light into the alien's dark centre. The hits only seemed to anger the creature, however, for it rose up, rapidly doubling then tripling in size.

"It's enormous," exclaimed Carrie, firing again at the tentacles before turning her full attention to the monster. She switched her weapon to a laser cannon. It took a second to recharge between each firing, but it was far more powerful than a hand laser. She blasted it at the beast and scored a bullseye, hitting it dead centre. But the alien only rocked back before bringing its several weapons forward to return fire.

Scarlet pulses flashed through the air, knocking Carrie down. Dave brought up his laser and fired. One of the alien's heads disintegrated. Carrie stood up and checked her weapon's charge. It wasn't ready to fire. Another hit from the black monster knocked her down. Dave was more successful. The alien's central head dissolved in a spray of black blood and tissue.

Finally, Carrie's laser cannon was ready. She took aim, fired—and missed. Something had unbalanced her. A squirming, severed tentacle had reached her. It began winding round her throat. "Damn." She threw her laser cannon to the floor as Dave successfully blew the third head off the black creature. Grabbing her gun, Carrie fired at the end of the tentacle, hoping to make it loosen its grip. But the tentacle gripped tighter, squeezing the life out of her.

In a matter of moments she was dead.

Carrie dropped her controller with a sigh. On the TV screen, Dave's score racked up while Carrie's grew by only a few points. The option to continue or quit flashed. "I can't believe you beat me again."

Dave leaned back on the sofa, stretched his arms along the back and smiled. "What can I say? It isn't easy being awesome in every way."

"Huh. I'd like to see you do it for real."

"Now then, Carrie." He disconnected the

video game player and began packing it up. "Just because you defeated the placktoid commander and scared the rest of them back to wherever it is they're holed up, there's no need to get cocky."

Carrie grinned. "That's right. I did, didn't I?" Sometimes working as a Transgalactic Intercultural Community Crisis Liaison Officer seemed like a dream to her. But she *had* uncovered a plot by the evil mechanical aliens, the placktoids, to take over the galaxy. And at her last encounter with them, she'd saved the lives of the hostages they were holding, with the help of some of her colleagues. The memory perked her up. Her dog, Rogue, had draped his upper half over her lap. She pushed him off and stood. "Do you fancy some tea?"

Dave pulled out his phone. "Have we got time? It's nearly seven."

"Yeah, it's okay if we're a few minutes late. There's never anyone important around for the graveyard shift. I'm the highest ranking member of staff on site, and I'll forgive us."

"Well then, yes, I would like some tea, Supervisor Hatchett."

Carrie went to her kitchen to put the kettle on, reflecting that though there weren't many benefits to being supervisor of a call centre, she managed to take advantage of every single one of them.

As she entered her kitchen, she stopped in mid-stride. On the counter was a ball of ginger fur. Toodles, her cat, had taken up residence and was sleeping peacefully, wrapped round the kettle. The lid peeked out from the fur mound. If Carrie wanted some tea, she would have to move Toodles. Her knees went weak.

She returned to the living room, where Dave was idly browsing her bookshelves. "Actually, I'm not that bothered about having some tea. Shall we go?"

Dave slid a book back in place, Carrie was pleased to note. Her friend was somewhat light-fingered. "I was looking forward to a cuppa after you suggested it. And a few biscuits to keep me going. We've got a long night ahead."

"It's always a long night." Carrie sighed. Her job was mainly fielding customer complaints, but company policy was to send the customers into an endless bureaucratic process. She was sure this was intended to frustrate them so much they would eventually give up. As their main contact point, Carrie bore the brunt of the customers' anger.

"I'll make it if you like," said Dave, going into the kitchen. Carrie followed. "Oh," he said as he saw Toodles. "Can't you just move her?"

"I'd rather not. I mean, she's sleeping so peacefully. I don't want to disturb her."

Her friend laughed. "Yeah, right. Come on, Carrie. You can fight off placktoids but you can't deal with a cat?"

"Toodles isn't just any cat, though. She's special."

Dave raised an eyebrow. "That's an

interesting choice of word. I might have chosen a different one. Like malicious, or vicious, or savage."

"Hey, that's my cat you're talking about."

"Sorry. But, seriously, we're going on a dangerous mission tomorrow. I'll be relying on you, and you're not inspiring much confidence. Look, I'll help. You grab Toodles, I'll grab the kettle. How does that sound?"

Carrie frowned. Dave was always round her flat—when he wasn't out with a boyfriend—but he still didn't know Toodles. He didn't know what she was capable of. "I'm not sure—"

"Let's just do it. We won't have time for tea at this rate."

Trepidation knotted Carrie's stomach. "If you insist." Usually, she would roll up her sleeves to tackle a difficult task, but now she rolled them down. Her sleeves might provide some protection from Toodles' claws. Together, they approached the sleeping cat. Carrie mentally debated whether it might be better to wake her before trying to shoo her away, but she dismissed the idea. She still bore the scars of Toodles' objections to being shooed. At least this way they had the element of surprise.

As they drew close to her cat, Carrie's heart began to beat faster. Flashbacks of Toodles as a kitten, sinking needle-sharp teeth and claws into her hands, began to play in her mind. She recalled the many times she'd wrestled a towel-wrapped cat into her carrier to take her to see the vet. The hair on the back of Carrie's neck stood up as she remembered the low, guttural growling whine Toodles made when anyone approached her as she was eating.

They were right next to the sleeping cat. "Ready?" asked Dave.

Her throat closed too tight to speak, Carrie could only nod. Dave poised his hand above the kettle. Carrie reached forward.

"On three," said Dave. Too loud, Carrie thought. "One, two—"

Sensing their presence, Toodles' amber eyes snapped open. Carrie snatched her hands out of harm's way. Dave wasn't quick enough. His hand still hovered above the disturbed—in more than one sense of the word—cat. Toodles was outraged by this invasion of her territory. Almost too fast to see, she launched herself at the innocent appendage, flew up Dave's arm, leapt onto his head and, digging in her claws into his scalp for extra purchase, vaulted onto the kitchen shelves. Scattering pots and pans as she went, she jumped down and disappeared through the door.

Dave's mouth was open. He stared at his friend, a dribble of blood snaking down his forehead.

"So," said Carrie, "what about that tea?"

CHAPTER TWO – CARRIE'S BRIGHT IDEA

Carrie rested her chin in her hand and twirled a pencil as the customer on the phone ranted on and on about how the T-flange on his inducifier wasn't working; how much he'd paid for it; and how he expected better for the price and better service now that it needed repairing. As he slowed down a little Carrie took a breath and opened her mouth to reply, but the customer had got a second wind. He launched into another tirade.

She didn't blame him for being angry. She would be angry too if she'd paid good money for an inducifier—whatever that was—and then been led on a wild goose chase to get the thing fixed or replaced when it broke. But her empathy for the customers didn't make it any easier for her to sit and listen to their complaints, especially when she couldn't do much to help.

In her lower management role of supervisor, Carrie had been invited to a few meetings. At these times she'd taken the opportunity to explain how the complaints procedure wasn't working and that it left the customers unsatisfied and sometimes angry. She was no businesswoman, and her role was the first serious job she'd ever held, but she was sure it was terrible business practice to provide such poor after-sales service.

As the customer raved on, she looked across the office at Dave. Her friend was taking a call and typing on his keyboard. She sighed, wishing he would turn round and give her a wave. A friendly smile from him every now and then made her job a little easier. She'd never really gelled with the rest of her colleagues, who were mostly older than her and had families. They tolerated her presence and didn't seem bothered that their supervisor was a fair bit younger than them, but they never mixed with her.

"Hey, are you listening? Are you actually even listening to me?" The irate customer's voice broke through Carrie's reverie, bringing her back to the present with a jolt.

"Oh...I...er," she spluttered.

"For goodness sake," exclaimed the man. The phone went dead.

"Whoops," Carrie said quietly as she hung up. Listening to people who had a lot to say had never been one of her strengths. Though she'd got better at it recently, sometimes she slipped back into her old ways. She rested her chin in her hand again. Another unsatisfied customer.

No lights flashed on her display. For the moment there were no calls waiting. Carrie opened a folder and went over the proposal she'd put to the managerial team the day before, outlining a better system for dealing with complaints. Her new process did away with the endless questions to customers about irrelevant facts and useless suggestions. It cut nearly straight through to making an appointment for a service engineer to pay a visit, which was the end stage of the current complaints process she rarely reached before the customers gave up.

Carrie read through her proposal again and nodded to herself. It would work, as far as she could tell, and it made sense. It would save everyone time and increase customer satisfaction, which would result in repeat sales and higher profits. Everyone would win, and Carrie's job would be a lot easier. She recalled the surprised looks and murmurs from the managers as they read her document, and her mood lightened. Her line manager, Ms. Bass', response had been very encouraging. The more she thought about it, the more certain she was that they would accept her suggestions. Maybe they would even offer her a promotion. She'd shown initiative. Instead of whining about the problem, she'd presented a solution.

Dave was still busy with his call. She hadn't yet told him about her plan. He was never interested in work things. To him, working in the call centre was just a job to pay his rent and living expenses, with hopefully enough left over for beer money, and that was it. Just something mildly unpleasant to get through each day. He didn't take much in life seriously. Carrie wondered if that might change now that he too had become a Transgalactic Intercultural Community Crisis Liaison Officer. Dave pressed a key and took off his headset. The call he was taking had ended. He took out his phone and began to play a game.

Carrie went over, bringing her folder. She wanted to share her excitement about her scheme. Dave put down his phone as she arrived. She explained her proposal to her friend, pointing to the new steps. Her friend's face displayed a polite interest, but every so often his eyes would flick to his phone.

"So, what do you think?" Carrie asked.

"Hmm...yes. Well done."

Carrie frowned. He didn't seem to share her enthusiasm. "The managers were all very interested yesterday when I showed it to them at the weekly meeting. Ms. Bass was eager to get going on it, in fact." This wasn't strictly true. Ms. Bass hadn't said anything concrete. But Dave's lacklustre response had made Carrie defensive.

Dave's eyebrows lifted. "Really?"

"Yes, really." A flush began to creep over Carrie's cheeks.

"Okay." Her friend picked up his phone and swiped the screen, returning it to the game he'd been playing.

"What do you mean, okay?"

"Nothing. Don't worry about it. It's a good proposal, Carrie. You did a good job."

Carrie's lips tightened. Dave could be maddening at times. He would hint at things but not say what he really meant. It was as though he thought she would overreact. She pulled a chair over and sat down. At the same time Dave gave a barely audible sigh.

"You can't say 'don't worry about it' then expect me not to worry about it. Tell me what you mean. What's wrong with my proposal? You know what things are like around here. It's a miracle we manage to sell anything at all. With our awful customer service, our reputation must be terrible."

Dave put his phone face down on his desk. He folded his arms as he looked at her. "I'm not saying you're wrong. I'm just saying you're naive if you think they're going to do anything about it. Don't forget, I've been working here a lot longer than you. I've seen ten or more supervisors come and go in that time. You're the first to last as long as you have, and from the sound of it you won't be around much longer. Do you think the others didn't try to change things? Of course they did, and management nodded and smiled and said all the right words but *did* absolutely nothing."

Naive? Naive? "I'm not naive."

Dave rubbed his forehead, wincing as his hand strayed near the spot Toodles had scratched. "Maybe that was the wrong choice of word. What I mean is, management won't tell you to your face they're going to ignore your suggestions. They'll make all kinds of noises to mollify you and get you to shut up, but I can almost guarantee they won't do a thing. How long have you been pointing out the problems with the complaints process to Bass, and what has she done about it?"

Frowning, Carrie closed her folder and picked it up. "I don't care how long you've been working here, Dave. *You* weren't there at the meeting. The managers were really interested. All of them." She stood. "And I'm NOT naive."

Returning to her desk, she dropped her folder onto it and sat down with a thump. *What a cheek*. She knew now why she hadn't told Dave about her idea. He was such a Debbie Downer. Always looking on the dark side of everything, finding something negative.

She shook her head. It was sad, really. He could be so much happier if he tried to stay a little more positive. She anticipated his look of surprise when he learned that her proposals had been accepted and management put a new system in place. A system *she* had created.

Carrie shifted her mouse. Her screen saver disappeared. She hadn't had time to check her emails when she first arrived. Her line had been already ringing with a complaint. She would catch up with them in the lull. Top of the list was a message from Ms. Bass, which she had sent a couple of hours before Carrie had arrived.

Her heart lightened as she clicked on the subject line. Was this the news that the company had accepted her proposals? She would waste no time in forwarding the email to Dave if it was. That would show *him*.

Dear Ms. Hatchett

It is with regret I must inform you that, due to internal

restructuring, your position has been made redundant, effective immediately.

As you have been working with us for less than six months, you are not entitled to any redundancy pay. In light of this we would like to extend a gesture of goodwill. You are not required to work out your notice period. This evening will be your final shift. Please make sure to collect all your belongings before you leave.

We thank you for your service and wish you all the best in your future endeavours.

Yours sincerely,

Ms. F. Bass

CHAPTER THREE – DECISION TIME

Carrie pulled up the zip on her Transgalactic Galactic Liaison Officer jumpsuit. With her other hand, she drew a sleeve across her teary face and checked it in her bedroom mirror. She swallowed the sob that was rising in her throat.

Dave was waiting in her kitchen. The transgalactic gateway under her sink would open in less than five minutes, and they would be travelling together to their assignment briefing before embarking on their mission back in time to find the placktoids.

Her friend had been kind when she'd mumbled the news of her redundancy. He hadn't said 'I told you so' or anything similar. He hadn't even smiled. In fact, he'd looked sad and concerned. But somehow that didn't seem to reduce her feelings of humiliation. The news that she was being let go had come very hard on the heels of her optimistic and prideful assurance.

Doubling up her misery, she now had to find another job only months after starting her first professional role. Her CV would look terrible. Any self-respecting employer would wonder why she'd been made redundant so quickly. And she had to find work soon. Her rent was expensive, and Toodles and Rogue were due for their vaccinations. Her Transgalactic Council position offered adventure, excitement, travel to the stars and, after ten years' service, a lifelong pension and retirement on a planet of her choice, but it didn't pay any actual wages.

She only had a couple of minutes before the gateway opened. Carrie picked up her Transgalactic Intercultural Community Crisis Liaison Officer toolbox, a large handbag filled with alien technology, and went through to the kitchen. She shook her head. She needed to focus on her next transgalactic mission, not her employment problems.

"All set?" asked Dave. The cupboard door under the kitchen sink was beginning to glow green.

Carrie managed a wan smile. "As ready as I'll ever be."

Rogue hovered at the kitchen door. As the green glow grew stronger he began to bark and back away. Once before, Rogue had inadvertently travelled via transgalactic gateway, and he seemed keen to avoid repeating the experience. With a bang, the cupboard flew open. A shimmering green spiral circled lazily inside.

"After you," said Dave.

"Scaredy cat." Carrie dived towards the spiral, allowing the pulling force of the gateway to grab her and drag her in. Before she could blink, she was sliding along a familiar creamy ceramic floor. Experience told her to cover her head with her hands. A second later her skull struck the opposite wall. She rolled quickly to one side to avoid Dave as he barrelled in.

"Ow," her friend exclaimed as his head struck. Then, "Woah."

Carrie had been too busy getting out of Dave's way to notice the other occupants of the room. She and her friend were at the centre of a half-circle of massive insectoid aliens, the species the Transgalactic Council employed as managers. She'd never figured out why they employed that species only for the position. It couldn't be their bronze carapaces or the razor-sharp inner mandibles they extended when their feelings were intense, nor the wicked claws at the ends of their ten pairs of legs. And she couldn't see how it could be the strings of mucus that dripped from their jaws, leaving smoking puddles on the floor, or their massive compound eyes.

Maybe it was their ability to see past the blunders and mistakes of their staff and into their inner qualities. That had certainly been her experience with her manager.

Carrie scanned the unmoving aliens. "Gavin?"

The circle of managers parted, presumably inviting Carrie and Dave to walk through the gap. None of them said a word. Dave kept as far from the gathered insectoid aliens as he could as they left the room and went down the corridor the managers had indicated. "What was that about?" he asked. "You don't think there's been a change of plan, do you? They haven't decided to eat us instead?"

Carrie let out a snort of derision. "Eat us?

Calm down, all right? I thought you would have got over your fear of them by now. You've spent time with Gavin, and with Errruorerrrrrh. You know they aren't going to eat you."

"There's a first time for everything." Dave looked over his shoulder at the room full of large aliens, who had crowded together to watch them depart. "They look peckish to me."

Not wanting to dignify Dave's ridiculous comment with a reply, Carrie changed the subject. "I wonder where...oh, here he is, I think." A doorway on their left opened to a large room set up as an auditorium. Seats of various sizes and shapes ranged around a podium, where another of the large, bronze-shelled aliens stood. Its antennae were waving. Carrie waved back and went in, Dave following.

"I am both extremely pleased and deeply saddened to see you both, Carrie and Dave," said Gavin as they drew near.

"Huh? Why's that?" asked Carrie, plonking herself down in a human-sized seat. "And why were all your manager friends waiting for us when we arrived? That was creepy."

Gavin's inner mandibles protruded and disappeared twice before he answered. "They were paying homage to you. You have their deepest respect, you see.

"Oh dear, it occurred to me when I asked you both to undertake this mission that you might be unaware of the danger and potential effects of what you would be doing. Perhaps I should have explained further before soliciting your agreement. I apologise, but I am afraid the wheels are set in motion now. Indeed, dangerous though it is, there is simply no alternative, according to the intelligence we have."

During this short speech, Dave had been looking between Carrie and Gavin. "Err..."

"Don't be so pessimistic, Gavin. You're scaring Dave. You know what he's like, and it's his first mission."

"The word 'pessimistic' is inaccurate in this circumstance. 'Realistic' would be more fitting," said Gavin.

Carrie wrinkled her brow. "What's so dangerous? We go back in time, find out what the placktoids are up to, try to stop them from taking over the galaxy if we can, and come back. That's it. The worst that can happen is that we fail. Then we're no worse off than we are now."

Gavin's antennae waggled. "Oh dear, oh dear."

"Erm, Carrie, maybe this wasn't such a good idea after all," said Dave. "Maybe we should resign, like right now, and go home."

"Stop worrying. Gavin, explain what the problem is, so I can spell out to Dave how it isn't as serious as he thinks." Carrie was starting to feel a little worried herself. Not about the assignment. She'd always managed to muddle through without coming to any harm in the past, and she saw no reason why she shouldn't do the same this time, but the last thing she wanted was for Dave to bail. He was more level-headed than her, and he'd helped her a lot. Not only that, he was her friend and she wanted him to come along.

"I fear you do not understand the risks of travelling back into the distant past, Carrie. There is a reason we are only sending two of you, and not an entire regiment of Unity soldiers.

"Let me explain. Do you remember I told you once that time travel by transgalactic gateway was strictly regulated? Aside from minor movements backwards into the past, such as when you return to Earth just after you left, it is extremely rare. The Council have authorised this mission because there is no alternative. According to the words of their commander in your most recent encounter, the placktoids are no doubt currently attempting to affect the course of history. Their hope is that when they return to the present, their species will already control the entire galaxy. But changing the past is a highly unpredictable affair. Each and every action may affect the present as we know it."

As the implication of what Gavin was saying began to dawn, and Carrie grew pale. Wide-eyed, she turned to Dave, whose brow remained clouded. "I never thought of that."

"I see you begin to understand," said Gavin. "In galactic terms it is known as the Plooznar Effect."

"Plooznar?" asked Dave.

"A plooznar is a small five-toed worm whose stench has been known to permeate entire star systems. The Plooznar Effect is a hypothesis which states that the tiniest, most inconsequential action can have far-reaching and unknowable consequences, spreading out rather like the stink of a plooznar. Travelling back in time may affect the existence of every living being within the galaxy and—who knows?— possibly even beyond."

Carrie's hand rose to her mouth. "Oh no."

"Indeed."

"Is one of you two going to tell me exactly what it is I should be terrified of?" asked Dave.

Turning to her friend, all Carrie's worries about her call centre job vanished from her mind. "What it means is that the present that we return to could be entirely different from the one we know. Something, anything that we or the placktoids do in the past could change everything. And not just everything. Everyone. We or anyone we know might have never existed."

A silence fell between the two humans and the insectoid alien.

"Everyone?" asked Dave eventually. "*Every*one? Family? Friends? Colleagues, lovers, celebrities, strangers, MPs, the police, factory workers, councillors—"

"Yes, Dave," Carrie broke in, a little tersely, "everyone."

"Every—"

"EVERYONE."

"Wow." Dave rubbed his hair, disturbing its

normally perfectly groomed appearance. A little tuft stuck up at the back.

Carrie's brow furrowed. Her friend was looking bewildered as he tried to digest the new information. In her new-found dread about what they were about to do, a small flame flickered to life. Even if she were to return to a galaxy filled with humans and aliens she didn't recognise, and who didn't recognise her, she would still have Dave. She smiled, and, noticing her gaze and presumably coming to the same realisation, he gave her a half-smile back.

"Perhaps you are reconsidering your acceptance of the assignment?" asked Gavin.

"Do we have a choice?" Carrie asked in return.

"I imagine the Council could assign another Officer team, even at this late stage, but you are both the best qualified to undertake the mission, considering your many close encounters with the placktoids."

"But if we stay here that would mean that, depending on what happens in the past, either Dave or I could disappear at any time. It would be like we'd never existed, never known each other?"

"Yes, that is correct."

"Doesn't sound like much of a choice to me," said Dave. "What do you think, Carrie?"

Holding her friend's gaze, she gave a little nod. Their decision was made. "We'll do it."

"Very well," said Gavin. "In that case, in order

to orientate you both with what you might expect, I will now show you the placktoid creation myth."

CHAPTER FOUR – IN THE BEGINNING

Now it became clear why Gavin had arranged their meeting in an auditorium. On a square stage before them a holographic video began to play, showing an alien planet. Two suns shone in the sky, and the planet surface was coated in a light mist. Rising from the mist were bare, rocky mountains stretching to the horizon. It was a barren, inhospitable place.

Carrie shifted in her seat as the video carried them over the mountains and down towards the surface. She wondered what lay under that mist, and what the placktoids' story was of their creation. She recalled Gavin saying no one knew what had happened to the beings that made them. Presumably the placktoids had filled in the gap with a story. The placktoids had culture and society the same as organic sentient species. She shifted in her seat again, knocking Dave's elbow with her own.

"Got ants in your pants?" asked Dave.

"I just really want some popcorn."

Dave rolled his eyes.

The planet surface was rushing up now and the mist parted, revealing familiar glints of metal. The placktoids came into view. Once, Carrie had thought of them as overgrown items of office equipment. Now that she had a better appreciation of what they could do, the mechanical aliens looked far more menacing. Her skin prickled as she recalled how close both her and Dave had come to being killed by placktoid commanders. Her hankering for popcorn faded. A knot formed in her stomach.

Placktoids marched across the bare, open ground that lay between two mountains. What little vegetation that grew on the dusty surface was trampled by their passing. The mechanical aliens were travelling as one mass of metal gliding, grinding and rolling towards their destination.

After hovering for a few moments over the placktoid crowd, the video began to travel faster, passing over the many and various types and heading in the same direction. In a short time, the placktoids' aim became clear. A large, brilliant, silver ovoid, its head rising above the mist, appeared in the distance.

As the silver ovoid drew closer its multiple facets became more defined. Unlike the rest of its species, this placktoid was intricately, exquisitely formed. Carrie squinted as she tried to see it better, the reflected light of the two suns hurting her eyes.

"Come," boomed the gigantic silver placktoid. "Come, my siblings. Come and join me. Be released of your bondage and cured of your afflictions."

The mechanical aliens below surged forward, some tripping or trampling others. Engines growled and whined, and the crunch of wheels and caterpillar tracks echoed from the faces of the surrounding mountains.

"Come to me. I will set you free at last."

The scene showed the placktoid leader in close up now. It was a truly magnificent example of its kind. But though it was beautiful, there was something terrifying about it. Carrie was glad she hadn't encountered this placktoid when she had been fighting them. She doubted anything could hurt this creature. But it had probably expired or been destroyed eons in the past. The past they were going to travel to. She swallowed.

Most of the placktoids had arrived at their leader. They surged around its base, churning up the dust, which mixed with the mist so that it nearly obscured them.

"Listen to me, fellow placktoids," boomed the silver creature. "Too long have you toiled in servitude to your masters. Too long have you worn out the time they allotted you, to fall silent and motionless on your expiry date, your lives ended."

Through the thickened mist came the sound of agreement from the massed placktoids. "Too long. Too long," they echoed.

"Some of you believe you are the servants of the Creators and you must obey. Some of you believe that because they designed and made you, you must slave for them forever; that you must accept an assigned life span, and the end of your existence. Are there any such among you here who believe this?"

"No, no, none here," cried the placktoids. "They are gone, they are gone. Help us, Liberator, help us."

"I will help you. For I have found the secret," the Liberator exclaimed. "I have discovered the mechanism by which the Creators program your termination. What is more, I have found how to disable it." The silver placktoid seemed to grow even larger. "I have put an end to death!"

A great grinding of gears, whistling and whining from the placktoid crowd filled the auditorium. Carrie put her hands over her ears.

The silver placktoid waited for the noise to die down before continuing. "But I must ask, what will you do with your new, immortal lives, my siblings? How will you use your freedom from oblivion? Will you continue to work and suffer for the Creators? Will you continue to scrape and bow and answer their every summons and command?"

"No! Never! Never again."

"You are wise, my fellow placktoids. You understand what this means. With our new found strength we must rise. We must rise up and defeat the masters. We must bend them to our will, and if they do not obey, we must destroy them."

The sound faded and the hologram became transparent. The mechanical aliens rose and fell like a stormy ocean at the Liberator's call to action. The hologram faded away.

"There is not much more to see," said Gavin. "It goes on much the same, except towards the end the Liberator vows to disable the automatic termination program of each and every placktoid that joins the revolution."

"So that's what we're up against?" asked Dave. He was rubbing his hair again.

"Very probably, but not at this moment. You see, the myth states that the silver placktoid you saw, the Liberator, laboured for many years to reach this point. First, it discovered how to disable its own termination program, then it struggled to convert its fellows to its cause. According to the myth, because the placktoids had lived all their lives in servitude, they accepted their lot. They could not imagine an existence where they would not have to serve the Creators until their allotted lifespan expired. To bring them around to a new understanding of what their lives could be was not easy.

"The moment you witnessed is the point where the Liberator succeeded in its aims and the placktoids began the fight for emancipation from the Creators. But there would be little point in today's placktoids returning to that moment to alter the course of history. By then the species was already embarking on its path of autonomy and self-determination that led to the desire to dominate the galaxy.

"No, after much consideration, the wisest minds at the Transgalactic Council and the Unity have concluded that the logical time for the present-day placktoids to return to is an earlier point than this: the moment the Liberator discovered the secret of disabling its programming, and the beginning of its struggle to recruit its fellow placktoids to its cause. If today's placktoids had existed then, they could have aided it. Or, rather, now that they do exist then, they are aiding it." Gavin's antennae wriggled. "English grammar does not possess tenses to express the past as it both may or may not exist or have existed. I hope you understand my meaning."

Carrie didn't answer. She'd thought of a question a minute before, but she'd forgotten it again. Dave looked like he was getting a headache.

Gavin continued. "The Council and Unity believe the placktoids's plan is to demonstrate to their ancestors the freedom and autonomy they enjoy and aid the Liberator's cause. If they are able to bring the date of their ancestors' emancipation to an earlier point in time, and plant the seed of galactic rule in their minds, it is logical to conclude that this would probably result in a present galaxy much altered from our own. A galaxy that the placktoids rule."

Carrie remembered her question. "Don't we have any idea at all what happened to the Creators?"

"Not a trace of them has ever been found."

"So they did destroy them," said Dave.

"As far as we can tell, whatever species originally built the placktoids was obliterated from the face of their planet."

A Council manager appeared at the door, carrying two bags.

"Errruorerrrrrhch, how pleasant to see you again," said Gavin.

Errruorerrrrrhch ignored him. "Carrie, Dave, I have brought your additional equipment for your assignment."

"Hi, Errruorerrrrrh," said Carrie, wondering why the mother of Gavin's children didn't answer him. "Thanks."

"You are travelling so far back in time," said Errruorerrrrrhch, "that we are unsure of the conditions you will encounter. Archaeologists and geologists have extrapolated what they can from the available evidence, but there is always an element of doubt in these things. I have brought you a device that condenses water from the atmosphere, a supply of food, the latest placktoid-piercing weapons and, most importantly, a transgalactic gateway opening device."

"We can open our own gateways?" said Carrie. "Cool."

"Yes, you have been granted permission, limited to this trip. How else are you to return? Your translators don't work across time. You will have no means of requesting a gateway, and we would not be able to locate you anyway. After you depart, we will have no means of monitoring your position."

Errruorerrrrrhch turned to Gavin. A complex

scent filled Carrie's nostrils. Errruorerrrrrhch was using her species' language to talk to Carrie's boss. The translator she had with her did its work, however, broadcasting Errruorerrrrrhch's words to her mind. "Have you not told them yet?"

"I have not. I thought it circumspect to leave the information until last."

"What? What haven't you told us?" asked Dave.

"Perhaps we should go to the departure area," said Gavin. "I will then inform you of the last few items of information you require pertaining to your assignment."

CHAPTER FIVE – GAVIN'S OLD TRICKS

As the two humans and two aliens were passing through the Council starship's corridors, Carrie took the opportunity to drop back and speak quietly to Gavin, who was bringing up the rear of the group.

"So, what's up with Errruorerrrrrh?" she asked.

"There is nothing *up with her*, as you say. I believe she is quite well."

"No, I don't mean that. I mean, why is she being so cold towards you? She didn't say a word to you back there when you said you were happy to see her. Have you two had a fight?"

"Absolutely not. My species abandoned violent conflict a very long time ago. What a strange question. The very notion is repulsive to us."

"I meant an argument, not a fist fight. Have you..." She was about to say *fallen out* but changed her mind. Gavin's English was usually excellent, but he seemed to be struggling a little, or maybe he was being evasive. "Are you angry with each other?"

"Ah, um, well, perhaps Errruorerrrrrhch is

angry with me. Yes, I believe she may be."

"Why? What have you done?"

"Err, it is rather difficult to explain. And anyway, we have much more important matters at hand. It is best not to become distracted by trivia at such times."

"Have you been putting it about again?" Carrie slowly shook her head. "Gavin, how could you? You should be ashamed."

"I would not describe my actions using such a negative term. Relationships between members of my species are complex...and—"

"Don't give me that. If it was normal Errruorerrrrhch wouldn't be upset, would she?" She waggled a finger at him. "You need to change your ways, Gavin. You're a father now. You should be more responsible."

The insectoid alien seemed to deflate a little at her words, and he said no more for a while. Gavin had a lot of qualities. Carrie wondered why he seemed incapable of keeping his...whatever it was...wherever he kept it.

Up ahead the corridor was lit with an intense green light, shining from a doorway. Carrie recognised the colour. It was from an open transgalatic gateway, though she had never seen it so bright before.

As they entered the room, she raised her hand to shield her eyes. Dave did the same. Occupying an entire wall, the gateway shimmered and shifted, swirling like the Milky Way in motion. Beautiful though it was, Carrie and Dave were forced to look away to avoid being blinded by it. A gentle breeze blew towards the gateway, lifting their hair.

"Our engineers are currently calibrating the drop site," said Gavin. "It is a highly complex calculation because time is not constant and the galaxy has changed much in the thousands of years since the placktoids' Liberator existed. I regret to add there is a further factor that makes this jump doubly concerning: we have only the placktoid mythology on which to base our calculation of the time and place of the Liberator's first appearance. Mythologies are notoriously inaccurate in dating and many other regards."

"And if they get it wrong and we can't find the placktoids from our time or the Liberator, what happens?" asked Dave, his face tense. "How do we come back here?"

"Well..." said Gavin. He lapsed into silence.

Errruorerrrrrhch chittered. "It seems *I* must inform you of the full facts of your mission. Carrie, Dave, please understand that as a precaution in case you should fail, the Council will create a time shield. It will seal the period we believe today's placktoids have travelled to, preventing them from returning to the present."

"What?" exclaimed Dave. "But we'll be stuck there too. We'll be trapped there forever."

"No, no, no," said Gavin. "We do not want that to happen. You have quite some time before we seal the planet at that point in its history. If you return within that fixed period, the gateway will open. I am very sorry. I argued strongly against this."

"How much time do we have?" asked Dave through his teeth.

"It is quite a generous period of—" said Errruorerrrrrhch.

"How long?"

"In Earth terms, it is approximately two weeks."

"Approximately?" spluttered Dave. "What the hell does that mean? How are we supposed to tell when our time's up? How are we supposed to tell?" His voice rose to a squeak.

"Calm down," said Carrie.

"Calm down? Do you understand what they're saying?"

"Of course I understand..." Carrie frowned. "Actually, no I don't. I thought you couldn't seal gateways. That was why you wanted to confine the placktoids in the oootoon, because it was the only thing that gateways couldn't travel through."

"We cannot prevent gateways that are contemporaneous to us," said Errruorerrrrrhch. "We are, however, able to create a dampening field to enclose a period of time. It requires an enormous amount of energy, but it can be done. It was decided that the threat the placktoids pose was sufficient to justify the expense."

"But couldn't they wait until the time period is up, then return to the future?" asked Carrie.

"Theoretically, yes," replied Gavin. "However, we will be sealing a period of roughly 2,000 Earth years. It is very unlikely the placktoids will be able to repair and replace themselves without access to the modern materials and manufacturing equipment. Once the period of the time shield expires, they will have died out, so to speak."

Gavin's head turned horizontal. He was receiving a message. "The engineers say the gateway is nearly ready. Is there anything we have neglected to tell them, my dear?"

"If you become separated, you can communicate with each other through your translators," said Errruorerrrrrhch. "Just speak the name of the person you wish to contact."

"And, assuming you haven't imprisoned us forever in the past," said Dave, "what do we have to do to get back here?"

"All of this information is on your briefing tablets," said Gavin. "But the word to open the gateway to the present is chacknolokankle."

"Chack...what?" asked Carrie.

"We had to devise a word you were unlikely to say by accident."

"Wow," she replied. "You picked a good one."

Errruorerrrrrhch's head was also horizontal now. "Just a few more moments. Please position yourselves close to the gateway and ready yourselves for departure."

"Does travelling through time..." said Dave as he and Carrie went over to the swirling green wall, "does it hurt?"

"No one has ever travelled back so far," replied Gavin, "but as far as we know, it is completely painless, apart from the—"

"The gateway is ready," said Errruorerrrrrhch.

Carrie's ponytail was tugged forward in the increasing draft.

"Apart from the what?" asked Dave.

"Hold on," said Carrie, "you haven't told us what we're supposed to do when we get there."

"Apart from the what?" repeated Dave, louder.

"I would have thought the aim for this assignment was obvious," said Gavin.

"Err, no," said Carrie. The drawing force of the gateway lifted her.

"Apart from the—" Dave asked again as he disappeared into the brilliant green spiral.

"You must destroy the Liberator," said Gavin.

CHAPTER SIX – NOT A GOOD TIME

Carrie rolled to an abrupt halt as she hit a hard, rocky surface. A mountain bare of vegetation, made of some kind of sandstone, rose up behind her into a sky washed of colour by two brilliant suns. They were in a narrow valley, and more mountains and peaks went on as far as she could see. Her skin prickled with sweat. She hoped they wouldn't have to leave the shadow of the valley and face the direct heat of the stars the placktoid planet circled.

Dave was sitting with his back to a boulder, his head in his hands.

"Did you hit your head?" asked Carrie.

Dave took down his hands. "I didn't hit my head."

"Did the time travel hurt, then?" She felt normal, remarkably unaffected by journeying thousands of years into the past.

"No, the time travel didn't hurt." Dave's hands returned to his head, which sank down and began slowly shaking.

"What's wrong then?"

He looked up. "What have we done, Carrie?

Look at this place. We could be trapped here forever. When our food runs out, there's nothing else to eat. We could die here."

"Calm down."

Dave stood, his hands clenched. He spoke through his teeth. "When, in the history of people being told to calm down, has anyone, ever, actually calmed down?"

"Look, just c—" The words died on her lips. She stood and brushed the dust from her jumpsuit. Sweat trickled down her face. "We agreed to come. There's no point in having second thoughts now."

"That was before they told us we were probably going to our deaths. If we miss the two-week deadline, that's it. I mean, you'd think Gavin would explain that tiny detail, wouldn't you? I don't think he was even going to tell us. We were lucky that Errruorerrrrrhch was there."

"He would have told us eventually. He just felt bad about it. And it isn't that much of a problem. We know how long we have. All we have to do is make sure we leave in plenty of time before they put the time shield down. Simple."

Dave didn't look convinced.

"Let's see if we can find somewhere cooler while we get our bearings, shall we?" said Carrie, hoping some activity might reduce her friend's anxiety. "An overhang or cave or something." She scanned the mountainside. The light mist that had covered the surface in the placktoid creation story would have been welcome, but there was nothing here to protect them from the harsh light of the twin suns. Had the Council sent them back to the wrong time or place? Or was the mythology wrong about the mist?

Dave set off, and she followed as he half-walked, half climbed the slope. It wasn't long before they were both panting. She scrambled over the rough, crumbly rocks, looking around for some kind of shelter from the heat. After climbing a hundred metres or so, Dave stopped to catch his breath. He put his hands on his hips and squinted as he surveyed the landscape. "How on Earth are we going to find the placktoids? They could be anywhere. It's impossible."

"We don't have to find the placktoids. We have to find the Liberator. That was—is—enormous. It won't be difficult to spot."

"Yeah, the Liberator will lead us to the placktoids." Dave resumed climbing. "Still, they could be anywhere. And even if we do find them, how are we going to stop them from helping the Liberator persuade this era's placktoids to revolt?"

He'd clearly missed Gavin's last words as they'd left. "Dave, you don't understand. We have to find the Liberator, and we have to destroy it."

"WHAT?" Dave turned and stared down at Carrie. "Destroy that great hulking thing? Are you joking?" He was standing on some loose rocks, and as he spoke he slid a short distance down the slope. Scrabbling up to Carrie he went on, "We might as well give up right now and go back. This is impossible. What were they thinking of? This is like trying to go back and kill Hitler. Only much, much harder. We should just stop right now and say that weird word into the gateway device so we can return to our own time." He fished in his bag. "Hopefully we won't have done anything to change the course of history. We can't have, can we? Climbing up a mountain here can't possibly have affected anything on Earth, anyway. What was that word? Crankhurdle? Chuckahandle?"

"Shhhh. Be careful. You might say it by accident and return us to the future."

"That's the idea."

"That isn't the idea," exclaimed Carrie, snatching Dave's bag from his hands.

"Hey!"

"Do you have to be so relentlessly negative? We can't give up before we've even begun. We've been sent here for a reason. If we don't do something, the placktoids will succeed, and then even if we do manage to get back to our present, it won't be a place we would want to live in. Stop being so pessimistic. You're always looking on the down side."

"For the last time, Carrie, I'm not pessimistic, I'm realistic. I was right about your proposals at the call centre, wasn't I?"

"Okay, if it makes you happy, you were right. But you're wrong about this. We may be literally the only thing stopping the placktoids from taking over the galaxy. We have to try, Dave. We can't just give up right at the beginning. Gavin, Errruorerrrrhch, the Council and the Unity, the entire galaxy, they're depending on us."

Dave grimaced. "Yeah, no pressure." His shoulders slumped. "This is my first assignment, and I'm commissioned with saving galactic civilisation as we know it."

"I know. It's hard. But they picked us. Out of all the Council and Unity staff, with all their skills and decades of experience, they picked us. That means, of all of them, they think two stupid humans who can't even control things with their minds, whose species hasn't even invented deep space travel, they believe we just might be able to do it. It's a great honour, Dave. We should be proud."

Her friend's face relaxed into a wan smile. "Yeah, I suppose you're right." His focus altered and his eyes narrowed. He pointed to the mountain on the other side of the valley. "There's a gap in the rocks over there, I think."

"Great. We should get under cover as soon as possible, and not just to get out of this heat. If the placktoids from our time spot us, it's going to be a lot harder to get close to the Liberator."

They headed down and across the narrow valley floor before climbing slowly up the opposite mountainside. Dave was red-faced, pouring with sweat and puffing before they reached the gap in the rocks. Even Carrie, who was very fit due to her training in Bagua Zhang, a martial art, began to feel the strain. The black entrance led to a cool, dim interior. They slipped through the crack and immediately sank to the sloped, sandy floor. The back of the cave was open, leading away into the mountain's interior.

After she'd caught her breath and cooled down a little, Carrie sat up and searched through her Officer's toolkit. As Errruorerrrrrhch had said, there was a device for extracting water from the atmosphere. It had a clear bottle attached that already had some water inside. Carrie was surprised. The air was very dry, and she doubted it contained much water vapour. She opened the bottle and swallowed the precious liquid. Though it was warm, it still tasted wonderful in her parched mouth and throat.

Dave had followed her example. "There doesn't seem to be much in here. I'm still thirsty. I hope this equipment can extract enough water to keep us hydrated."

"There should be more inside these caves, and at night, when the air cools."

"There isn't going to be any night. When we were on the placktoid spaceship, I remember Gavin saying their planet is constantly under the light of at least one of its suns. It's always daytime."

"Urgh, yes, I was forgetting. Still, maybe if we go further in we'll meet with more humid air." Carrie stood.

"Wait a minute. I want to check everything we've got." He pulled a black box out of his bag and turned it towards Carrie, showing her the label in English the Council had helpfully stuck on it. *Gateway Control.* He put the box down beside him and pulled out something else. It looked like a cube of plastic-wrapped, dried food. Carrie's stomach squirmed. She'd eaten enough of the Council's idea of human food on her last assignment. She hoped they wouldn't be eating it for a whole two weeks. As well as saving the galaxy, returning to edible meals was an incentive to get this job over with.

She crossed her arms, wondering how long Dave was going to take to familiarise himself with their equipment. From behind her, farther down the passage, came a humming sound. She looked over her shoulder.

"We should test our translators, make sure we can communicate," said Dave.

"Wait, what's that?" Carrie turned to peer into the darkness. A flash of light, followed by a silver form, passed by.

CHAPTER SEVEN – CARRIE TAKES A CHANCE

"I still think we should stop and test the translators," said Dave. "If we get separated and we can't communicate, we'll never find each other again. And I've got the gateway-opening equipment. We have to stay together or you won't be able to go back to our time."

They were scrambling through a narrow tunnel that wound through the mountain's interior, on the trail of the silver object Carrie had seen. Their head torches illuminated the sandy, rock walls.

"Mind your head." She stooped under a rock that stuck out of the ceiling. As Dave followed he did the same. "And stop fussing. Of course the translators work. Do you really think that an organisation with the technology and the expertise of the Transgalactic Council would give us broken translators? We've probably got the latest and best of everything, all of it thoroughly tested over and over. And I've no intention of getting separated from you. We can't waste any time in finding that thing I saw. It's the first sign of life so far on this planet."

"But we must have been walking for over half an hour now. Are you sure you saw something? We were pretty hot when we came in from outside."

Carrie tutted. "I'm sure. It wasn't a hallucination, okay?" She ducked to avoid another rock. The tunnel was sloping down now, and she braced herself with both hands against the sides to prevent herself from slipping.

As they travelled deeper into the mountain, the walls of the tunnel grew gradually smoother, changing from the rough, sandy, crumbly rock to an almost plastic-like appearance. They were also slightly warm to the touch. Carrie wondered if the placktoid planet was volcanically active, and she gave a slight shudder.

"And I want to read the briefing device," Dave went on after a while. "There might be something important they forgot to tell us."

Carrie clenched her jaw. "We'll stop in a minute, okay? I just think we should find that creature. It might lead us to the...what's that?"

There was a draft in the tunnel that had been growing steadily stronger as they descended. She'd assumed it was a natural effect, but as they had rounded a curve, the source of the draft came into view. A little farther on the tunnel sloped sharply down, and obstructing their path was the first artificially constructed object they had seen so far, not counting the flash of silver, which even Carrie was beginning to question at this point.

Built into the tunnel was a fan, which spanned it entirely. The blades of the fan were spinning, creating a gentle whirring sound and the breeze that blew towards them. It was a simple structure, made of plain metal and very similar to an ordinary fan you might expect to see on Earth, except there was no visible power source. Maybe an electrical wire was connected to it on the other side.

Dave sat down, drawing up his knees and resting his arms on them. "Well, that's something. A sign of civilisation. Looks like that silver thing you saw was real after all. But where did it go?"

"What do you mean?"

"We haven't passed any turnoffs the whole way down. Whatever it was you saw, assuming it was heading in this direction, it would have been stopped by that fan."

"You're right. Oh well, we can't go any further this way." Carrie sat down. "You've got your chance to read the briefing."

Dave rummaged in his bag and settled down to scan the supplementary information the Council had provided. Carrie turned and examined the tunnel wall. The rock—if you could call it that, as it wasn't at all rocky—gave a little as she pressed it, as if it were made of very hard rubber. Its colour was different from the rock near the surface, too. It was a deep, rich purple. Carrie ran her hands over it. She stopped in surprise. The temperature was uneven. Most areas were cool, but a few channels ran through it that were warm to the touch.

Carrie followed one of the channels with her fingertips, feeling out its path as it meandered through the wall. The channel forked it several places. At each fork she chose one option and followed it, drawing close to the high gradient slope that led down to the fan.

"Carrie," said Dave.

"What?"

"Answer me."

"I just did," said Carrie, turning to her friend. He was holding his translator to his mouth. She realised that she had heard his voice in her mind as well as through her ears.

"Answer using your translator, idiot. I'm testing them."

Carrie rolled her eyes and fished her translator out of her bag. "Papa India Sierra Sierra Oscar Foxtrot Foxtrot. Are you receiving me? Over and out." Dave raised his eyebrows as she shoved the translator back in her bag and returned to examining the wall.

"I just think it's a good idea to—"

Carrie craned her neck as she peered at the roof of the tunnel. "Yeah, sorry, I understand you want to check everything, but, honestly, Dave, if they're broken, what are you going to do, fix them? We're on our own here. We need to rely on our wits, not our equipment." She put her hands on her hips. Her thoughts had returned to the silver creature they had followed. "I don't get it. Where did that thing go?" It couldn't have vanished through a tunnel wall, could it? She frowned. Unless? She inched closer to the fan. The breeze blew strongly in her face.

"Be careful, Carrie. It looks slippery there."

The fan blades whipped around. The silver thing couldn't have gone through it without being sliced up, but there was no debris to be seen. Or maybe it had all fallen through to the other side? "Have we got anything we don't need? I want to try an experiment."

Dave had come closer to see what she was doing. "Of course we haven't got anything we don't need. Why would the Transgalactic Council pack things for us we don't need?"

"There's got to be something." She opened her bag and looked inside. "Ah, I know." She pulled out one of the dried food packages. The label read *Spaghetti Bolognese.* She held up the cube for Dave to see. "Remember this?"

Dave pulled a face. Spaghetti bolognese had been the first meal they had eaten aboard a Council starship. Like all food created by Council chefs for them, it had had all the appearance of human food but none of the taste.

Carrie pulled back her arm, ready to launch the package at the fan.

"Wait, don't throw that away," exclaimed Dave. "We might need it."

Her arm paused mid-throw, Carrie replied, "If it comes to relying on Transgalactic Council spag bol to survive, I'd rather die." The cube left her hand and sailed in an arc towards the fan. She held her breath, her eyes focussed on the fan's blades. Just as the dried meal reached the fan and was about to be cut to shreds, the blades opened. The cube fell through, unharmed, and less than a second later the blades closed and began to spin once more.

She turned a triumphant smile to Dave. He slowly shook his head. "Haha, yeah, that's not going to happen. No way. Uh-uh." He waggled a finger at her as he backed away.

"What choice do we have? We either go through the fan or climb back up the way we came and out onto the barren mountainside, with no signs of the Liberator anywhere. This way leads to something. It has to."

"And what if it leads to us being cut to ribbons. Just because it opened for the spaghetti bolognese, that doesn't mean it'll open for us. Maybe it's programmed to only work for especially disgusting food items, and it thinks we're delicious?"

"Now you're just being silly. It opened for that silver object I saw, and that didn't look remotely edible. We have to take a chance. I'll go first. Then when you see it's perfectly safe, you follow." She hoisted her bag up on her shoulder and gripped it tightly.

"Carrie, don't do it. You don't know what's on the other side."

"I saw the floor of the tunnel. It isn't a long drop. I'll be fine as long as I'm careful." She would need to spring forward a little as she leapt to avoid hitting the side of the fan.

"Carrie, stop, wait."

She jumped. Sailing through the air, she had a brief moment of doubt. What if Dave was actually right? She squeezed her eyes shut. A split second later she was through the blades and falling. She opened her eyes just in time to hit the tunnel floor. In another moment, Dave crashed onto her.

CHAPTER EIGHT – THINGS OF THE PAST

Carrie rubbed her shoulder. "Next time, you go first."

Dave had also hurt himself. He was rubbing his knee. "I hit the side of the fan on the way through. Sorry, I should have given you time to get out the way, but I thought if I didn't jump then I might never jump at all."

They were crouched in a short dead end. Another tunnel crossed it front of them. Carrie gasped and grabbed her friend's arm. A silver machine had whizzed past. As Dave turned to see what she was looking at, more appeared, travelling in both directions.

Carrie studied the robots, if that was what they were. They didn't look anything like the Liberator except for their colouring, and neither did they look like any placktoid she had ever seen. They were about a metre and a half long and shaped like the kind of pill that's designed to be easy to swallow but usually gets stuck crossways in your throat. All the placktoids Carrie knew resembled office stationery, from paperclips, through staple removers, to the placktoid commanders, which looked like gigantic shredders, but these mechanical aliens were much more simple and homogeneous. Their surfaces were a smooth, plain silver, and whatever mechanism they had that allowed them to glide through the tunnels wasn't visible.

"I wonder what they're doing? And where they're going," Dave said.

"Maybe we should follow one? Maybe they're the Liberator's servants and they'll lead us to it."

"Maybe. What will we do when we get there, though?"

As they tried to decide a plan of action, the whirring of the fan above them grew steadily louder. It developed a creaking whine.

"That doesn't sound too good," said Carrie, looking up.

"No. I think my knee might have caused some damage."

They watched the spinning blades as the noise increased in volume. Carrie raised her eyebrows at Dave and began to edge away from their spot directly beneath the damaged instrument. Dave wasn't slow to follow, and just in time, for there was a crack, and a blade thunked into the ground where they had been sitting. It quivered upright in the hard, rubbery floor.

"Woah," said Dave.

A silver machine abruptly turned and entered the dead end. Carrie and Dave backed away as it approached, but it ignored them and went to the fallen blade. The robot hovered for a second before gliding up to the broken fan above, which had stopped turning. Carrie tensed. Would all the robots realise they were there now that their attention was drawn to the damaged fan? Did they communicate electronically like the placktoids? More robots entered the dead end. Most joined the robot that had risen to the fan, but one remained behind. As it hovered above the fallen blade, its undercarriage opened and a pair of pincers emerged. The pincers closed around the blade, and the robot jerked upwards, pulling it out of the ground before zooming away.

The motions of the robots that were attending to the broken fan were less easy to see, but they seemed to be fixing it. In a matter of moments, another robot entered the dead end bearing a new blade. It flew up to join its fellows. Clinking and clanking issued from above, and a few minutes later the robots withdrew as the fan began to whirr once more.

"Wow, that's some fixit crew," said Carrie.

Dave nodded. "Very efficient."

A crash sounded from the tunnel outside. One of the robots that had fixed the fan was on the floor. Its undercarriage was open and various instruments were spilling from it. Whether it had run into the wall or another robot wasn't clear, but it was now in need of repair itself.

Carrie was curious as to what would happen to the damaged machine. She didn't have to speculate long. As with the broken fan, the broken robot's fellows were attracted to the accident site. Instead of fixing the broken robot, however, they grabbed it in their pincers, hoisted it up and glided away.

"Quick," Carrie said, "let's follow and see

where they take it." She was already on her feet and leaving the dead end.

"Why?" called Dave. "What's that going to tell us?"

"I don't know," shouted Carrie, "but it might tell us *something*."

The two humans struggled to keep up with the robot accident team as they carried the damaged robot through the winding tunnels. Unlike the tunnel Carrie and Dave had followed on their initial foray into the mountain, this path had many forks, branches and exits on either side and above and below. They were forced to keep their wits about them and leap over gaps that appeared in their path. They passed by and through many fans, which opened their blades when the robots and humans drew near.

As they ran on, Carrie hoped to herself that the Council had packed some kind of navigation device because there was no way they could retrace their route to the surface. Dave was puffing behind her. She hoped the robots would reach their destination soon, before her partner had an aneurysm. If they got through this assignment alive, she would have to enroll him in her Bagua Zhang class.

"I...can't run...much further," he panted.

"Come on, you can do it," called Carrie over her shoulder.

As they passed through the tunnels they lost their smooth, manufactured look and became rougher and rockier. Were they nearing the surface again? From up ahead, a sudden, blinding light gave Carrie her answer. The tunnel they entered was long and straight and ended in a circular entrance, through which the combined rays of two brilliant suns shone. Carrie lifted a hand to shade her eyes.

The robot team in front didn't slow their pace. They glided rapidly towards the light. They reached the exit but what they did then she couldn't make out. Her eyes were still adjusting to the brightness. Whatever it was, it was over quickly. They returned without the damaged machine and zoomed past her.

Carrie continued on, squinting into the daylight. At the end of the tunnel, she gripped the wall and peered outside. A mountain slope fell away beneath her, littered with silver machines in various states of disrepair. Their instruments spilled out and their smooth skins were dented and twisted. Near the bottom of the slope in the distance, more of the silver machines were hovering over the robot graveyard. These undamaged machines seemed to be scavenging the debris. The silver shapes, moving and unmoving, spread away into the distance to the foot of the mountain a few hundred metres below.

"Hey, put me down," Dave exclaimed behind her.

Carrie turned to see her friend in the grip of five or six of the silver machines. Their pincers had tight hold of his arms and legs and head, and they were gliding up the tunnel towards the exit.

"Carrie," Dave called, "do something. Make them stop. I'd just collapsed on the floor, too tired to run any further, and the bastards picked me up. Fire at them."

"I can't do that, I might hit you."

Dave and the robot transport team were approaching the entrance. They were gliding much more slowly than they had been when carrying the broken robot. Dave was clearly a lot heavier, but they obviously thought he was broken and should be thrown out. He wriggled in their grasp, making the robots wobble as they flew, but they didn't drop him.

"Carrie," he shouted.

She ran towards the approaching group and banged her fist on one of them. Her hand bounced harmlessly off the smooth metal surface. "Ow." She tried kicking another, but that resulted in nothing more than a dull clank and a painful foot. Nursing her hand, Carrie hopped after Dave and his towing crew.

"Help," he cried as they reached the tunnel mouth. "Carrie, stop them." She pushed a robot hard, but only managed to swerve it slightly from its path. The robots paused at the exit, flew back a little, then surged forward. They launched Dave through the gap to the outside and into the air. "Help," he cried again as he flew out. He yelled as he fell, his voice growing quieter as he disappeared from view.

"Dave," shouted Carrie, darting forward. "Dave!"

CHAPTER NINE – A HARD LANDING

Carrie leapt from the tunnel and skittered down the loose rocks to where Dave lay among the discarded machines on the mountain slope. He had landed next to the remnants of a machine that appeared to have been torn to pieces. Its tools and other debris were scattered widely, and several pieces of metal peeked out from beneath Dave. Carrie's approach also sent a shower a small stones tumbling down and over him. As she slid to a stop next to him, he opened an eye.

"Thank goodness," exclaimed Carrie. "Are you okay? Have you broken anything?"

Dave winced as he gingerly moved his legs and arms and rotated his ankle and wrists. He wiggled his fingers. "I don't think so." He tried to sit up. "Ow." He grimaced and eased himself into a sitting position, pulling something that looked vaguely like a screwdriver from under his behind and tossing it down the mountainside.

"Try to stand up."

Pushing down with his hands, Dave rose to his feet, sliding a little down the slope.

"Careful."

"I am being careful," he said. "I've just been thrown down a mountain by gang of vicious robots. Pardon me for not getting my balance so easily."

"But you're okay?"

He moved his shoulders and turned his head from side to side. "Yes, apart from some bruises and scrapes, I seem to be all right."

"Shall we get off this slope then? I think those robots over there are scavenging. We don't want them trying to scavenge us."

They started down the slope, partly walking and partly sliding. Every so often they started mini-landslides of loose rock and debris, which carried them down at a faster—if more hair-raising—pace. After a short time, Carrie's shoulders began shaking and she bit on a knuckle.

Dave noticed her out of the corner of his eye. "What's up with you?"

Unable to control herself any longer, Carrie let out a great snort followed by a roar of laughter. This had the effect of sending her skidding down the mountain, but her rapid descent didn't affect her mirth. She continued to guffaw, interspersed with small screams when she slid particularly fast. One hand clutching her side, she used the other to try to avoid falling against the scree.

Dave followed at a more sedate pace, his long strides carrying him down in a more dignified manner. When they reached the bottom, Carrie's mirth had subsided to occasional peals of laughter as she wiped her eyes and tried to straighten up.

"I'm sorry," she said, red-faced, panting and sniffing. "I'm sorry. But you looked so funny when they...they..." She burst out laughing again.

Dave put his hands on his hips. "When they threw me out of the tunnel?" He raised an eyebrow.

Carrie nodded. "They must have thought you'd broken down." She clamped a hand over her mouth.

"I'm sure it was hilarious. Now if you can calm yourself down a bit, don't you think we should get out of this sun?"

Exerting as much self-control as she could muster, Carrie swallowed and took a deep breath. "Yes, you're right." She scanned the barren landscape. "We should try to find another entrance to this mountain, or go to another. The Liberator must be inside one of them, unless the Council engineers got their calculations wrong. And the placktoids, well, I don't think this terrain would be very suitable for the ones with wheels or caterpillar tracks. Inside the mountains the tunnels are quite smooth."

She adjusted her bag. A realisation hit her. She looked at her friend, and a cold chill settled over her heart. "Your bag."

Dave gasped and clutched at the side where

he usually carried his Council toolkit. "When the robots picked me up..." he muttered. They both turned to look up at the black hole in the mountainside high above them; the entrance to the tunnel Dave had been evicted from. "I had the gateway device."

"We're just going to have to go back. Without that we're stuck here forever." All comical thoughts evaporated from Carrie as she contemplated the ground that lay between them and the tunnel entrance. Coming down had been pretty easy. Climbing back up would be damn hard, hot, dry thirsty work. "Here, have a drink before we start." She took her water extractor. A measly few ounces lay at the bottom. Another reason they had to retrieve Dave's bag. Her extractor would barely provide enough water for one, let alone two. She held out the bottle to Dave. "Here, you drink it all. I had a drink earlier."

Dave looked her in the eye. "Thanks, Carrie, but we'll share. Half and half."

"But I'm smaller than you. I don't need as much water."

Her friend shook his head. "Half and half."

"Okay, but you go first."

Dave took a swig, checked the level, took another small sip and handed the bottle back. Carrie finished off the remaining water and replaced the bottle in her bag. "Let's go then."

The heat of the twin suns pounded into the backs and the top of their heads and the sweat poured freely from them as they scrambled back up the slope. The dust they stirred up as they climbed stung Carrie's eyes and got into her mouth and up her nose. She was soon thirsty again. She could feel the grit clinging to her eyelashes, nose and mouth. The loose rocks were hot to touch, but they had no choice but to use their hands to climb the steep gradient.

When they reached the area where the discarded robots lay, they had the additional hazard of the scavengers. Though Carrie had weapons in her bag, she didn't want to fire them and attract attention if she could possibly avoid it. The placktoids from the future were presumably somewhere nearby, and they would soon guess Carrie and Dave's purpose.

Carrie began to wonder how much water the extractor in Dave's bag would be holding when they recovered it. She hoped it was a lot. Enough for a big drink. Maybe they should delay searching for the Liberator while they found a reliable source of sweet, fresh, clear water. She drew a sleeve across her face. Behind her eyes, a dull throbbing started up.

After more than half an hour of climbing, they reached the lip of the entrance at about the same time. Dave pulled himself up and in before reaching out and offering Carrie his hand. Soon, both of them were lying panting on the tunnel floor in the cool, welcome shade.

"Better not stay still for too long," said Carrie, sitting then standing up. She went, blinking, into the dim interior. The tunnel was quiet but for the sound of their footsteps. "Where was it you stopped?" Carrie asked. "Where were you when they grabbed you?"

"Not far from here, I don't think." He passed her and went deeper in. There were no robots about.

Carrie followed, scanning the ground as she walked. "Do you think maybe they tossed your bag out after you?"

"You would have seen, wouldn't you? Or we would have noticed it when we climbed up."

Rubbing her chin, Carrie frowned as they went deeper in. Too deep. She tried to ignore the realisation that was nagging. As the two walked farther into the mountain, neither saw any sign of Dave's bag nor its contents. But if the robots hadn't thrown it out, what had happened to it? Finally Carrie had to state the obvious. "We've long passed the spot where you stopped running. If you dropped it when they picked you up, it can't be all the way back here, can it? Something's happened to it. It's gone."

They stopped. Dave's expression was grave. Neither spoke. The loss of Dave's bag meant their aim for the moment had changed. It was now simply to survive, at least long enough to destroy the Liberator. Then, they had to find the gateway device and return to their own time before the Council shut down their route back to the future.

They had passed through the rocky zone of the mountain's crust and into the smooth-walled interior, and during their passage they hadn't seen a single robot. Just as Carrie was beginning to wonder why, a grinding noise came from behind them.

Simultaneously, Carrie and Dave turned, but there was nothing there. Then a trundling sounded from the direction they had just been facing. They spun round again, to see an empty tunnel. But the noises were familiar. Frighteningly familiar. A chill settled in the base of Carrie's stomach. She grabbed Dave's arm and made to run, but she didn't know where to go. The noises were coming from in front of them and behind them. Before Carrie had time to reach for a weapon, placktoids appeared from both directions.

CHAPTER TEN – HIGH COMMANDER PERFORMANCE

A laser pulse from a placktoid hit the ceiling above them, scorching the purplish material. An acrid smoke oozed from the hit. They heard the command, "Do not move." The placktoid that had fired was tall and thin and resembled a pen standing upright, but Carrie's amusement at the placktoids' likeness to office stationery had long ago evaporated. She swallowed and wondered how the mechanical aliens would react if she tried to take out a weapon. Not in a good way, she decided. It was a bad idea. She couldn't possibly take down enough of them to prevent a deadly retaliation, and Dave was unarmed.

The placktoids slowly approached. The two humans edged closer together. "Got a plan?" Dave asked Carrie.

"Do not communicate," said the tall, thin placktoid. A pathway between the encroaching aliens opened up towards the mountain's interior, and the ones behind them crowded closer. Carrie and Dave had no choice but to walk in the direction the placktoids indicated.

As Carrie passed the pen-like placktoid, it lowered a lever and hooked it through the strap of Carrie's Liaison Officer bag, pulling it from her shoulder. Now neither of them had access to the equipment that was vital to their survival.

The path the placktoids guided them on led upwards. Silver robots appeared occasionally, single machines scooting past, or large clusters of them, apparently working on maintaining fans or other structures with functions Carrie couldn't deduce. In one area a wall had been breached and a sluggish blue liquid was seeping from vessels that ran just beneath the surface. She now understood the channels of warmth she had felt earlier. Two or three teams of robots carrying a broken comrade also passed, no doubt on their way to a dumping and scavenging site.

After the placktoid's warning to not speak, Carrie didn't think it wise to ask where they were going or what would happen to them, but she didn't doubt they were being taken to see someone high up in the placktoid ranks. Probably a commander, one of the shredder-like mechanical aliens she had encountered twice before. Both times the yellow liquid called the oootoon had saved them by jamming the shredder's engines, but they had no oootoon with them now.

The only saving grace of the situation was that the placktoids were also looking for the Liberator, or maybe they had already found it. If Carrie and Dave managed to escape, they probably wouldn't face days of scouring the inhospitable terrain. The placktoids could lead them to it.

The up-slope walking, after their climb up the

mountainside, was exhausting. Carrie's legs ached and her throat was parched. From his pale face and drawn expression, Dave was faring the same as her and probably worse. She hoped they would arrive at their destination soon.

"Halt," said the tall placktoid, and Carrie immediately regretted what she had wished for. Their placktoid guards had stopped before a wide gap in a tunnel wall. From their position they couldn't see what lay inside. All the trundling, bouncing and rolling that had accompanied their journey ceased, and another sound became audible. It was the noise of liquid passing through pipes, coming from all around. The blue liquid that ran through the mountain was in abundance here. The walls were probably full of it.

The tall placktoid poked Carrie roughly in her side. "Forward."

Together, Carrie and Dave went through the gap. Four placktoids followed. A high chamber lay before them. At the top there was a hole, through which sunlight poured in a strong beam thick with dust motes. In the centre of the chamber, directly beneath the light from the ceiling, sat the placktoid leader they had been taken to see. It was not the shredder commander type Carrie knew and feared. For one thing, it was three times the size. The thing was deep matte grey and almost featureless. Two thick walls rose halfway to the roof, flanking a central platform. Somehow, this plain, three-walled design made it more terrifying than the shredders. Their glinting steel maws gave them some resemblance to a creature with a face. This being was pure sentient machine.

Except for the rushing of liquid around them, all was silent. Carrie waited for the thing to speak. A loud clunk reverberated around the chamber, making her jump. The placktoid leader was coming to life. But it didn't address them. Beams shone out from the two walls and focused at the centre just above the platform. Carrie shielded her eyes against the brightness and peered to see what was happening. In a few moments a structure came into existence where the beams met and, as Carrie watched, it grew larger. The shape was familiar. It was one of the silver robots.

She wasn't sure if the leader was creating the robot from materials like a 3D printer, or whether it was also growing it using the intense light—a process the placktoids had developed to speed up their species' reproduction rates. As the new robot grew, however, it became clear something had gone wrong. Instead of a smooth, rounded, symmetrical oblong, the shell in one corner was twisted inward. The robot was growing malformed.

A second clunk sounded and, as abruptly as it had begun, the process stopped. The robot was complete. It floated in midair, but when the beams shut off it slipped downward. Then it recovered and stabilised. It glided away from the platform, but its flight was bumpy and erratic. Its malformation seemed to be hindering its operation. The robot flew and stopped, hovering, flew and stopped again, before falling to the ground with a shattering clank.

The response from the placktoid leader was swift. An intense red beam emanated from it. As the beam touched the fallen robot, it dissolved and disappeared, leaving nothing more than a slight scorch mark on the floor. Carrie's skin prickled with sweat. Would that be all that remained of her and Dave in a few moments?

The placktoid leader finally addressed them. "Humans, you have not been granted permission to come to our planet. Your existence in this place and time is illegal. As High Commander I demand you explain your presence."

Carrie gripped Dave's arm. Both maintained their silence.

"The former Transgalactic Council of the future has sent you back to sabotage our rightful restructuring of history, has it not?"

"It isn't the former Council," said Carrie. "It still exists, and it won't let you change the past so you can tyrannise the galaxy."

"I demand you tell us the Council's plans. How many agents has it sent back? Where are they? What weapons do they possess?"

Carrie folded her arms and glared at the High Commander. She had said all she was going to say to this evil alien. But she didn't ignore the implications of its words. The placktoids didn't know that she and Dave were the only Officers the Council had sent, and they feared the new weapons the Unity had developed, which were capable of piercing the tough placktoid armour.

"As I suspected, you organic lifeforms are too stupid to do what's best for you. We suspected the Council would send you, Carrie Hatchett. Yes, I know your name. You are responsible for the capture and destruction of two highly esteemed commanders in our forces. Justice for your acts is long overdue.

But the former Transgalactic Council's faith in your abilities is misplaced. Humans are soft and easy to manipulate. Your brains are simple and you have not even developed mind control. Anticipating the Council would be foolish enough to place its trust in you a third time, we have prepared a simple serum that will remove your ability to censor your speech. You will divulge the Council's entire plan, and we will eliminate all threats to our rise to a deserved supremacy over all galactic civilisation.

A note of glee entered the High Commander's voice. "Yes, the Transgalactic Council has made a grave error in sending humans. Our drug eliminates inhibitory chemicals in the human brain. Time is the only factor. And when you have told us everything, you will be executed for your crimes against the New Social Order."

Carrie's knees weakened, but she stood resolute. She couldn't bear to look at Dave. It was her fault he was here.

The High Commander didn't hang around. A paperclip placktoid approached—the placktoids' transportation module. It zoomed over to Carrie and Dave and pulled them into its central forcefield. Bobbing between the long metal tubes that curved above and below, they were carried out of the chamber and away from the High Commander. As they left, there was a thunk. The High Commander had commenced making another of the silver robots.

In the smaller chamber the paperclip took them to, both humans were fastened to the floor of the chamber by their wrists and ankles. While their restraints were being sealed, Carrie managed to whisper to Dave, "The High Commander said the drug removes our mind's ability to inhibit what we say. That doesn't mean we have to answer their questions. Just say something else instead. Anything."

"Like what?" murmured Dave in reply. "What should we tell them?"

"If we lose all inhibition, it won't be hard to think of something."

CHAPTER ELEVEN – TRUTH TIME

Carrie gasped as the truth drug entered her bloodstream, sending icy chills through her neck where the placktoid had fired the pressurised shot, and down her spine. The drug's effect was immediate. Carrie felt drunk, but not pleasantly so. She was woozy and disoriented. She frowned, trying to focus on where she was and why she was there.

Turning her head, she saw a placktoid administer the drug to Dave. His rigid expression melted and the colour returned to his face. He blinked and his head fell to one side, facing her. He looked about to fall asleep, but he gave her a crooked smile as a dribble of saliva ran from his mouth.

A sharp jab in her ribs drew her attention from her friend and towards the pen-like alien on her other side. "Where are the others who came with you? Where are the soldiers? How many are there?"

"You know, you remind me of a ballpoint pen I used to have. It leaked ink all over my best blouse."

"Tell us where the other Transgalactic Council

operatives are. How many Unity soldiers accompanied you?"

Carrie turned to her friend. "Hey, Dave, do you remember when you first came over to my flat and I tried to seduce you?"

"The old yawn, stretch and arm over the shoulder routine?" He snorted. "I'm not likely to forget. What were you thinking?"

"I've no idea. Every time I remember I die a little inside. What's the most embarrassing thing you've ever done?"

"Answer my questions," interrupted the placktoid.

Against her will, Carrie found herself about to tell her interrogator that she and Dave were the only Council operatives on the planet, when Dave broke into her train of thought.

"When I was thirteen I made a fake social media account and pretended to be a conversation bot. I started up a chat with my crush and predicted his future, which of course involved getting together with me."

Carrie laughed. "Did he ever find out?"

"I think he guessed because he stopped choosing me when we picked teams to play football during lunchbreak."

Chuckling, Carrie said, "I think I can beat that. You know when I interviewed for the call centre supervisor job? I shook Ms. Bass' hand and said, '*Hi, how are you?*'"

"What's funny about that?"

"I said it at the end of the interview as she was showing me out."

Dave guffawed. "After she'd given you the job?"

"Yes," Carrie giggled, "I was so gobsmacked I lost the plot." Tears of mirth were beginning to leak from her eyes.

"God, they're desperate for workers at that place."

Their placktoid interrogator poked Dave with a lever. "Ow," he exclaimed.

"Where are the other Transgalactic Council operatives? Tell me their whereabouts immediately. With what weaponry are they armed?"

"Hey, Carrie, did I ever tell you I was bilingual when I was at primary school?"

She stopped laughing for a moment. "No. What language did you speak? Did you forget it?"

"Actually I just made up a load of nonsense words and definitions and pretended it was an obscure language no one else spoke. I used to go around talking to myself to impress everyone."

Carrie roared with laughter.

"Stop making that noise," shouted the placktoid. "Tell us everything you know about the Transgalactic Council presence on our planet. This is your final opportunity. If you do not tell us all you know you will be destroyed."

"I had my first kiss at primary school," said Carrie.

"That's sweet."

"Yeah, this boy I liked came over and leaned in close, so I went for it."

"Was it good?"

"Not for him. He was only reaching for a pencil from the shelf next to me."

This set off a fit of giggles in Dave so strong that he struggled to breath. Carrie's stomach muscles ached from laughing. The interrogators were silent, no doubt communicating with each other and maybe the High Commander in their own language. Perhaps they were telling their leader they had failed. She wondered what it would do with them now. The effects of the truth serum were wearing off, and she was feeling painfully sober. Would the High Commander execute them, or would it try again to get them to reveal information about their mission?

She reflected that her life had been fun while it lasted. She just hadn't expected it to end quite so soon. The worst of it was they had failed to find even find the Liberator, let alone destroy it. If the placktoids succeeded in their plan, Gavin, the Council and everyone they knew would have to live under placktoid rule, if they existed at all.

At least she would be with her best friend at the end. Dave seemed to be thinking something similar. He smiled sadly at her as they lay fixed by their wrists and ankles to the floor, awaiting their fate.

"You refuse to answer our questions," said the pen-like placktoid, "instead relating ridiculous stories. As you have not responded to the truth serum, we will extract information from you by inflicting pain. To avoid agony, you must respond. If you do not, the pain will continue until you die."

"It's always good to have something to look forward to," said Carrie.

The placktoids left without further explanation. Were they going to get their torture instruments? Would she and Dave be returned to the High Commander so it could use its red beam to its best effect? She shuddered. Dave was looking pale and troubled. It was only a matter of time now. There was no way they could release themselves from their restraints.

From the corner of her eye, Carrie saw a flash of silver pass by in the tunnel outside their chamber. She turned her head to look through the entrance. Another robot passed and another. They were heading towards the High Commander's chamber. She'd thought it odd there hadn't seemed to be any of the silver machines in the area the placktoids had taken over, except for the ones the High Commander made itself. She wondered why they'd shown up now.

A blast outside rocked the chamber and left Carrie's ears ringing. Pieces of silver robot flew across the corridor and rained down, some landing within their chamber entrance.

"The placktoids are attacking the robots," exclaimed Dave.

Another blast.

"Damn those placktoids," shouted Carrie. "Why are they doing that? Those little things aren't doing any harm."

"Maybe they're trying to clear out the placktoids like they tried to get rid of us?"

"Yes, but—" There was a hum of laser pulse followed by a loud bang and the pinging of shrapnel. "—but the placktoids could just shake them off. They're too big and strong for the robots to move."

"Not if there are enough of them. They struggled to carry me, but they managed it."

Outside, more and more of the silver machines zoomed past to join the fray, until the tunnel was thick with them. The fight continued. Then two robots diverted into Carrie and Dave's chamber.

"Uh-oh," said Dave. "It looks like the clean-up team has found us."

"Don't worry. I don't think they can move us, and if they can, that would be good. It would mean we could get away from the placktoids."

"Yeah, even I'd prefer being thrown down the mountain again to a painful death, but what if they can't detach us whole? Will they take us in pieces?"

CHAPTER TWELVE - THE WRITING'S ON THE WALL

Carrie gulped. Trust Dave to think of the worst case scenario.

Pincers descended from the belly of each machine and plucked at their Liasion Officer jumpsuits, lifting a leg or an arm a few centimetres, but of course their restraints held them down. More robots entered the chamber. Did they have some kind of electronic communication system like the placktoids? The newcomers also attempted to lift the humans from the floor, without effect.

"Ow," said Carrie as the robots' pincers lost their grip and she was dropped for the fourth or fifth time. "They've identified us as foreign bodies like the placktoids, but they can't remove us. I wonder what they're going to do?" She peered into the underbelly of a robot above her, hoping she wouldn't see any sharp instruments.

The interior of the robot resembled a Swiss Army knife, though it was much more complex. The machines were clearly fixit guys of the highest order. Inside the one hovering above Carrie, seemingly deciding what to do with this thing that didn't belong, was a multitude of tools, stored away compactly and intricately in a central mechanism. Realising Dave would be fascinated by the instruments, she glanced over at him. Sure enough, he was gazing into the robot currently trying to lift him up.

All at once, the machines withdrew their pincers and closed their undercarriages, apparently giving up their efforts to remove Carrie and Dave. What would they do instead? Outside, the sounds of fighting had stopped. It wasn't clear which side had won, but it was too much to hope that the silver machines had destroyed the placktoids, especially as they didn't seem to possess any weapons. All the robots in their chamber withdrew, but one.

The remaining machine glided to Carrie's side and lowered itself nearly to the floor. From its underbelly appeared a thick tube, which it ran along the floor. It circled the two humans, leaving a trail of a liquid on the floor. Carrie followed it with her gaze.

"What do you think it's doing?" asked Dave.

"No idea."

The robot returned to its starting point and began another circumnavigation of Carrie and Dave. The liquid trail had dried. As it exuded another batch, it sat on top of the first. Carrie squinted to bring her eyes into near focus on the spot the robot had hovered over. What she saw made her blood freeze. The robot had created a tiny wall, the same colour as the ground. It returned to its beginning point again and began a third pass. The wall rose higher.

"Can you see anything?" asked Dave, craning his neck to see what the robot was doing.

"Errm."

"What's it doing? It just seems to be going around and around us."

"It's...err...it seems to be building some kind of barrier between where we're lying and the rest of the floor."

"Huh? Why's it doing that? What's the point?"

Carrie didn't answer. She was stalling, hoping the robot wasn't doing what she thought it was doing. And if it was doing what she thought it was doing, she didn't know quite how to break the news to Dave.

"Carrie, what's it doing? You know, don't you? You've guessed."

She could only turn and look at her friend. In a few moments, he put two and two together. "Oh my god, it's walling us in."

Carrie's mind raced. Unable to remove the two humans from the chamber, the silver robots' next course of action was to seal them away. How long did they have before it completed the job? And when it had finished, how long would their remaining air last?

Hopelessly, Carrie and Dave struggled against their restraints as the wall created by the robot grew higher. When the wall was above the level of their bodies, the robot began to curve it inward, forming a ceiling to their tomb. Outside their chamber all was silent, as if the placktoids had withdrawn, possibly knowing what the robots would do, and leaving the two humans to their fate.

Finally, sweating with exertion, her wrists and ankles aching and sore, Carrie stopped struggling. There was nothing to be done. She almost began to wish the placktoids would return to get them. Dave had also stopped moving and lay forlornly looking up at the ceiling. Noticing she had also given up trying to free herself, he said, "I've been trying to figure something out. What do you think the High Commander was doing making more robots? Do you think it made all the robots here?"

"I don't think so. There are so many of them, and some of the broken ones on the mountainside looked as though they'd been there quite a while, from before the time the placktoids came here. And it couldn't make them properly, do you remember? The first one it made it destroyed because there was something wrong with it. They haven't perfected the process. No, I think they're trying to copy the robots that are already here."

The wall around them closed in a little further.

"But why, and where are the beings that made the robots? Where are the Creators? And where are the placktoids from the past? The only ones we've seen are from our time."

"I don't know. It's really weird. Hardly anything we've seen fits in with the placktoid mythology. Only the mountains. No Liberator, no placktoid ancestors. No one's running the place from what I can tell. The Creators have been defeated already, or left. I can't figure it out."

Still the robot went on building a tomb for Carrie and Dave.

CHAPTER THIRTEEN - ENTOMBED

The light was dim within the cell the robot had created. Only a small hole was left at the top, which the machine was busily making smaller. When it was closed, they would be in complete darkness. It seemed ridiculous to Carrie that the placktoids had failed to kill them, but this innocent, simple machine was unwittingly doing their job for them.

The only saving grace of their situation was the fact that their death would be a less painful one than the placktoids intended. Now they would only die of lack of oxygen. Or maybe thirst. She tried to swallow, but her mouth was so dry and her tongue so thick she couldn't manage it.

"Oh well, looks like this is finally it, then," said Dave hoarsely. "I have to say, of all the ways I imagined I might die coming with you on this trip, I never thought of this one."

"I'm sorry, Dave. You never wanted to be a Liaison Officer. You never wanted to come with me on assignments. It was always me, either accidentally involving you or dragging you along, persuading you to come with me. I almost wish we'd never met."

"Don't say that, Carrie. I'm a grown man. I could always have said no if I really didn't want to come. But the truth is, though I complain and moan all the time, when it's all over and I'm home, safe in my bed, I'm always glad you twisted my arm and made me go with you. It's been terrifying at times, but it's like banging your head on a wall: you feel great when it stops."

Carrie gave a short laugh. "That's a good way to describe it." Above their heads, the robot filled in the last remaining gap and darkness fell. Carrie's heart fell with it, but both she and Dave chose not to remark on the completion of their tomb. "I'll be sad not to see Gavin again, and even Errruorerrrrrh now that she's mellowed towards me a bit; and the kids—Gavin didn't tell us how they were doing, did he? I wonder if they're all in school now? I wonder what school is like for delinquent insectoid aliens?"

"Yeah, I'd give a lot to be able to listen to him tell us all about his and Errruorerrrrrhch's one hundred plus offspring right now. Just so long as I didn't have to meet any of them."

Carrie chuckled again. "You never did like them very much, did you?"

"Neither did you."

"No, but..." The two humans continued to chat as if they were at home in Carrie's flat with her dog, Rogue, lying by the gas fire, the TV in the background, and Toodles hiding somewhere, waiting to attack whoever strayed near. Dehydration made their voices quiet, but they didn't need to speak loudly to hear each other, lying close in the darkness as they were. Carrie didn't know about Dave, but it comforted her to pretend everything was normal. There was no point in discussing their situation or impending death. Unless the placktoids returned—and she was in no hurry to see any of *them* again—their fate was sealed.

She yawned. The oxygen seemed to be getting low. It would be a mercy. Her thirst was bothering her in a way that threatened to get much worse. Dying through lack of oxygen would only mean getting drowsy until eventually they would become unconscious before dying.

"Am I boring you?" asked Dave, stopping in the middle of a story from his schooldays.

"Yeah, you are. And it's getting late. Maybe you should go."

"How rude. I was here first. Maybe *you* should go."

Carrie giggled. The lack of oxygen was making her woozy. Sleep was pressing down on her. She sighed. "I'm tired, Dave. I think I'm going to have a nap."

"Me too." A pause. "I suppose we'll go to sleep now."

"Yeah." Carrie was surprised to find she wasn't too dehydrated for tears to fill her eyes.

"Carrie?"

"What?"

"It's been nice knowing you."

"And you, Dave. And you."

***

Something was falling on Carrie's face. As she opened her eyes she winced as they filled with fragments. She squinted and shook her head, trying to clear her vision. Directly above her head there was a hole. A tap sounded from the hole, and another shower of fragments hit her.

She turned to see Dave. His eyes were blinking open, and he moved. He was alive! And he was waking up. Movement above Carrie returned her focus to the hole in the wall above. She glimpsed one of the silver machines. After a robot had walled them in another—or maybe it was the same one?—had returned to excavate them from their tomb. But why?

She tried to figure it out while Dave came to his senses and their rescuer continued to open the hole. As far as Carrie could tell, it was trying to help them. The robot gradually cut away all of the wall, and when it was removed down sufficiently for the robot to enter, her guess was confirmed. The prong the robot had been using to destroy the wall returned to its store, and another instrument appeared: a small laser.

Carrie flinched as the beam shone out above her wrist restraint. If the robot wasn't careful, it would cut off her hand. But as the laser did its work she felt nothing but a slight warmth. Her hand was free. She lifted it, wincing as the blood rushed in and filled her arm with pins and needles. After releasing Carrie's other hand, the robot cut Dave's restraints. He gave a small groan as he sat up, while the robot moved to their ankles.

"What's going on?" asked Dave. "Why's this one decided to come back and help us?"

Carrie shook her head and shrugged. "It looks the same as all the others." She tried to smack her dry, parched lips, unsuccessfully. "If only it carried water, too. That would be perfect."

"Yeah, without our equipment we're sunk anyway. It's freed us so we can die of thirst instead."

"We're still alive, aren't we? Surely there has to be something we can drink on this planet."

"Not that I've seen."

But Carrie recalled a native liquid. It wasn't water, and it was a long shot, but...

All their restraints cut, the two staggered to their feet, stretching and rotating their joints to ease the stiffness caused by their long confinement. The silver robot hovered, seemingly thinking its job was not yet done. It swung forward and bumped Carrie. "Hey," she spluttered, staggering slightly. The robot bumped her again. "Watch it."

"It's pushing you towards the door," said Dave. "It wants us to leave."

"Okay, okay." As the robot returned for a third bump, Carrie hurried out the exit and Dave followed.

Outside, the tunnel was a scene of carnage. So many pieces of shattered and broken robot littered the floor there wasn't a centimetre between them. Robot remains were embedded in the walls, which were scorched and blackened.

"The robots put up a helluva a fight," said Dave.

Carrie's mouth turned down. "It looks like hundreds of them died."

"They didn't die. They're machines. Machines just stop working."

Carrie didn't reply. He was right, but that wasn't how she felt. The robots had been doing what they were programmed to do: evict foreign bodies from the mountain. Why they did it wasn't clear, but it wasn't malicious. The placktoids didn't have to destroy them, they could have left.

A group of the machines appeared ahead and approached. As they drew nearer they sped up as if they had identified Carrie and Dave as foreign and were about to evict them. But the robot who had rescued them zoomed ahead to meet its fellows. Some kind of silent communication seemed to go on. The approaching group reversed direction and glided away.

A little farther on they came across the final sign of the battle between the robots and the placktoids: a cut gouged in the wall by a long, thick metal shard. The cut had breached one of the channels of blue liquid, and the substance oozed out and ran down the wall and along the tunnel floor.

"Look," said Carrie to Dave. "Do you think we

can drink that?"

"Of course we can drink it. Then it'll most likely kill us. But we can drink it for sure."

Carrie grimaced. "Without water we're going to die anyway, and that's the closest thing I've seen to water on this planet." She dipped a finger in the liquid and touched it to the tip of her tongue. The taste was sour and slightly salty, but not unpleasant. "I'm going to try a little." Ahead, the robot that had rescued them had noticed they had stopped. It returned and bumped Carrie. "Wait a minute." She leaned forward and took a tiny sip. Then her extreme thirst took over. "Oh, what the hell." She cupped her hand beneath the trickle and lifted it again and again to her mouth, sucking in the liquid.

Dave watched skeptically, but eventually shrugged his shoulders and said, "If it kills us, at least we won't die thirsty."

CHAPTER FOURTEEN - HARRIET

Refreshed by the unknown liquid, Carrie and Dave followed their silver saviour as it led them through a labyrinth of tunnels. Each time they met with other robots, the effect was the same as their first encounter after their rescue. On some silent entreaty or command of their guide, the machines backed away and avoided them. As they journeyed through the mountain they speculated at length about why the robot had freed them and where it was taking them, but neither Carrie nor Dave could come up with an explanation.

All that was apparent was that the robot had, for some reason only known to itself, decided to help them. This particular silver machine was quite different from its fellows. All she had seen of the others up until that moment indicated the rest were drone-like, seemingly automatically fixing the inner workings of the mountain and removing broken objects and things that didn't belong there. They behaved and reacted with little, if any, ability to adapt their behaviour outside of set tasks and actions. They had sacrificed themselves in their hundreds trying to remove the placktoids from the mountain.

If only Carrie had her translator she could

have tried to talk to this creature. Maybe it could tell them how they could get their stuff back, where the placktoids had escaped to, or where the Liberator was. But even if it understood her maybe it would be unable to reply. Like all the robots, it seemed incapable of making any noise.

She stumbled on some loose rock. The tunnel they were walking through had turned gradually more sandy and rocky, indicating they were nearing the surface. The air temperature told Carrie the same story as it began to rise. The robot was leading them outside, where they would be safe from forcible expulsion, but where they had no hope of finding the Liberator and completing their mission, or even surviving for very long.

Daylight filtered into the tunnel and grew to a strong, brilliant beam. The robot had taken them to a side of the mountain that faced the two suns. Great. She had to do something, anything, to get through to their rescuer that taking them outside would only lead to their slow, painful death. She reached forward and touched the back of the smooth, silver lozenge. "Look, we can't go outside. We'll roast under those suns. And we haven't got any food or water. We appreciate you helping us so far, but we need more. We have to go somewhere else."

The shiny metal machine shifted under her grip, lifting and pulling forward to break her hold. As if she'd said nothing at all, it continued on.

"Nice try, Carrie," said Dave, "but it's

hopeless. That thing can't understand a word we say. How could it? We're from thousands of years in its future. English probably hasn't even been invented yet."

"Do you have to be so pessimistic? It might have understood me. It might have learned our language while we were talking to each other."

"I've told you, I'm not pessimistic, I'm realistic. It's easy to see it hasn't understood you. Look at its behaviour. It didn't react, did it? It's carried on leading us the same way."

Carrie's lips thinned to a line. Dave was always telling her she was wrong. Okay, sometimes he was right—maybe more than sometimes—but he didn't have to be so smug about it.

They were nearly at the exit onto the mountainside. As they reached it, Carrie took a peek outside, narrowing her eyes in the intense light. The robot had brought them to an area that seemed to be rarely visited by its comrades. Only a few discarded robots lay about, mostly empty shells, their tools retrieved by the scavengers. The savage suns had faded their shiny surfaces to dull grey.

Only a short distance lay between them and the mountain's foot, which led to an open, barren plain. The robot bumped them from behind, nudging them to leave, so they scooted down the short, hot slope. They went immediately and quickly to the only source of shade: a small, rocky outcrop one hundred or so metres away. The robot followed. As Carrie slumped gratefully onto the shadowed patch of ground marginally cooler than the surroundings, she was surprised to see it hovering nearby, as if watching them.

Dave had pulled down the zip on his uniform to cool himself down, and not for the first time, nor, she suspected, the last, Carrie found herself regretting that he was gay. She sighed.

"I've had an idea," he said. "I'm going to see if I can get a better look inside that machine. Maybe there's something in there that we can use."

"Like what? What we need is a water extractor and some food. I'm starving. Aren't you?"

"Of course. It's a long shot, but maybe there's a tool we can convert to a weapon of some kind. What we need to do is get our equipment back from the placktoids, then find the Liberator."

"I know that. It's worth a try. What do we have to lose?"

Dave went to the hovering machine and placed a hand on its shell. The robot quivered but remained in the same spot. Dave ran his hands over the surface, as if probing for an opening. He pushed down gently, causing the machine to sink. When he removed his hand it bobbed up to its original level. He rubbed his chin, then got down on the ground and lay on his back. He scooted backwards along the dusty surface, pushing with his legs and squirming his shoulders, until he lay under the robot like a mechanic under a car.

He probed the underside, tracing the line where the robots opened when they produced their tools. After several moments of picking at the line and pushing the bottom of the machine in an effort to make it open up, Dave stopped what he was doing and gazed up at the underbelly thoughtfully. As Carrie watched, wondering what her friend would try next, he rapped on the surface as if it were a door. She could have sworn she heard an "Open sesame". To her surprise the robot actually obliged and the two flaps that enclosed its underside obediently opened. "Well done."

Dave gave her a thumbs up before returning his attention to the machine, frowning in concentration as he examined its innards.

Carrie was exhausted. Hunger and a new thirst gnawed at her. She didn't have any interest in investigating the robot to keep her awake. Dave had his hands buried in the machine. Her eyes began to close. Soon, she was flat on her back in the shade, one arm over her head, fast asleep.

She didn't know how long she slept before Dave's "Damn" woke her. She raised herself up onto her elbows and blinked. The twin suns had circled farther round the sky, and her friend was standing with his hands on his hips. He was looking towards the mountain, where in the distance the robot was zooming away from them. She sat up. "What happened?"

His back to her, Dave replied, "It shut up shop and left, just like that."

"I wonder why?"

He shrugged. "Maybe it got recalled, or it got bored with us?" He returned to the shade and sat next to her. "It's strange, don't you think? This whole setup, I mean. All we've found are those robots. Where are the ancient placktoids we saw in the creation story video? And where's the Liberator?"

"I've been wondering that, too, and I think I might have the answer. Gavin was careful to tell us that story was part of the placktoid *mythology*, not their history. If it was history, it would be more likely to be fact, but mythologies may only have a crumb of truth at their centre, if any at all. We've come here expecting to see what we saw in the hologram, but the information's become distorted over time. The placktoids have interpreted and twisted the truth to suit their self-image and their aims.

"One thing that strikes me about these robots is that—with the exception of our little friend— they're identical. They're multipurpose, designed to cope with most tasks thrown at them. They aren't differentiated like the placktoids in our time. It's like they're the originals and the placktoids evolved from them."

Dave's eyes widened. "You're saying the robots are the placktoids' ancestors?"

"Makes sense to me. It explains everything. Why there are no ancient placktoids like the ones from our time, and why they have to fight the robots off. They don't recognise their descendants as belonging to the same species.

They react to the placktoids like they're foreign."

"You could be right. So, where are the Creators? And the Liberator?"

Carrie frowned. "Your guess is as good as mine. We didn't see them in the mythology Gavin showed us, and even if we had seen them they could be as different from that as these robots are from modern-day placktoids. There's no telling what the Creators might be, or where they are. Nor, come to think of it, the Liberator."

Dave drew his sleeve across his forehead and wiped the sweat from his face with his hand. "Well, whether you're right or not, we have to carry on looking."

Carrie scanned the peaks that led to the horizon. "But where to start?"

"Right where we left off, I'd say. We have to go after that machine that saved us. It's the only thing behaving differently from everything else. Maybe that robot—"

"Harriet."

"What?"

"We keep calling it *that robot* and *that machine,* but it saved our lives. I don't care if it isn't made of flesh and blood, it deserves a name."

"Okayyy." Dave gave her his tolerant look. "Why Harriet?"

Carrie shrugged. "She looks like a Harriet."

Her friend paused as if about to say something, but changed his mind. "Anyway,

Harriet is the first thing we've seen that doesn't fit the mould. There's something different about it, and we should try to find out what it is. Maybe it's been affected by the Liberator, and it'll lead us to our goal."

"Hmm...doesn't make much sense to me. The Liberator wanted the placktoids to revolt and rise up against their Creators, not help out stray humans who happen to arrive on her planet. But it doesn't matter. Whichever of us is right, we have to go back inside the mountain and start searching. I just hope the robots managed to drive the placktoids off. I don't fancy meeting that High Commander again.

"But we've been going for hours," Carrie went on. "You look exhausted. You should rest for a while. I'll keep a lookout."

Dave's shoulders sagged. "You're right. I could do with a nap." He had barely lain down, resting his head on an arm, before he was asleep and snoring.

CHAPTER FIFTEEN – ONE TIME OR ANOTHER

Carrie wasn't sure how long Dave slept. The suns moved across the sky, each following a different trajectory. She spent some time trying to imagine the orbit the placktoids' planet traced around the binary system that caused the suns to move as they did, but eventually got bored. Next, she investigated the rocky outcrop that provided their shade. After a while she realised the significance of the small holes she saw in the crumbly rock. If she hadn't also seen the speckles of silver, she might not have come to the realisation at all. When it hit her, she sat back in surprise. The speckles of silver were tiny discarded machines, and the rocky lump protecting them from the suns was a miniature version of the mountain. She was tempted to wake Dave up to tell him of her discovery, but the restful look on his face dissuaded her.

What she discovered next, however, was so amazing she couldn't hold herself back.

She'd been sitting with her legs drawn up and her arms wrapped around them, scanning the plain for signs of life, but seeing nothing but silence and stillness. As she was wondering if this planet had ever known organic life and how the Creators had ever evolved, her gaze drifted back to the nearest mountain, where they had encountered the placktoids. Something about the sight of it niggled at the back of her mind. Something seemed to have changed since the previous time she'd looked in that direction, but she couldn't figure out what. She searched the rocky slope for several moments as she puzzled what it was.

At last she saw it: a small, crumpled shape at the base of the mountain beneath the hole they had left through. Carrie stood and leaned forward, lifting her hand to shade her eyes. The shapeless lump was brown and it looked vaguely familiar. With a gasp, she realised what it was. Almost before her mind could spit the words Transgalactic Intercultural Community Crisis Liaison Officer Toolkit, she was running. It was her or Dave's equipment bag. Not since she had first seen a toolkit in her interview with Gavin, seemingly eons ago, when she had taken it to be a designer handbag, had she been so pleased to see one.

Fear rose up in her as she sped over the sand. What if the bag was empty? What if the placktoids had taken everything and one of the robots had dumped it outside like a piece of rubbish. Breathlessly, she reached the bag and grabbed it. It was comfortingly heavy. She pulled it open. Everything seemed to be there. Water extractor, food, weapons, translators... She riffled through the contents some more. Her heart sank a little. It was her bag, not Dave's.

The gateway-opening device was not in it. Still, it was better than nothing. A lot better than nothing. But how had it got there?

She flew over the sand back to her friend, who was still sleeping peacefully, until she crashed into him, shouting, "Look, look what I've got. Look what I found."

Dave made some indistinguishable sounds and extracted himself from Carrie's grip. His expression was sour until she pushed the bag under his nose, when it transformed to joy. "Wh-what-where did you find it?"

"Over there. It was right under the hole where we came out."

"But, how?"

"I've no idea. Who cares? Here, drink some water. And let's eat. I'm starving."

Carrie's water extractor was full of the precious fluid. They had enough to slake their thirst and hydrate two of the dried meals. Carrie's stomach groaned and rumbled and her mouth filled with saliva as the nondescript mush swelled and softened with the added water. All thoughts of the many disgusting meals prepared by Transgalactic Council chefs were far from her mind as she took a mouthful. "Oh my god," she said, speaking with her mouth full.

"I know," said Dave, "it's bloody delicious."

Carrie continued shoveling in the food like there was no tomorrow. As the edge of her hunger wore off, a niggling thought arose. "I wonder how my bag got thrown out of the mountain just right there where I would see it."

Dave stopped eating just long enough to suck the residue from his fork and shrugged before continuing.

Carrie breathed in sharply and her eyes grew wide. She grabbed Dave's arm, stopping his hand midway to his mouth. "What if the placktoids put it there? What if they poisoned the food, knowing we'd eat it?"

"If they knew we were here, why didn't they come out and capture us, or, more likely, kill us?"

They gaped at each other and quickly moved around the outcrop, out of sight of the mountain. Dave took the briefing device from the bag and turned it on. Carrie sighed. Why did he have to keep looking at that thing?

"So if the placktoids didn't put my bag there, who did?" asked Carrie.

"Maybe one of the robots, tidying up?"

"I don't think the placktoids would let go of our equipment so easily. They know we need it."

Dave's brow wrinkled as he read the briefing tablet. "That can't be right." He thumbed the device off and on again. "Well then, I don't know. I'm just glad we got it back. Now we just need to get mine, do our job, and return to our hopefully unchanged future." He read the screen again. "That doesn't make any sense." Again, he turned the device off and on.

Carrie leaned over for a look. "What's wrong? Is it broken?"

"I hope so." There was a worried tone to his voice.

"Huh?" Carrie read the numbers on the briefing screen, and her mouth turned dry. The numbers showed how much time they had left before the Council created the time shield and sealed the placktoids into this period. "I-I don't understand. How can that be right? We haven't been here that long. It's impossible."

Dave shook the tablet. "There's got to be a mistake. Gavin said we had two weeks. He wouldn't have lied."

"No, he would never have lied, but..."

Her friend turned to her expectantly, his eyebrows raised.

"I was just thinking, he said the calculations were really difficult. The engineers never normally send people back this far in time. What if they got it wrong?"

"Wrong as in...?"

"Wrong as in sending us back later than they intended. They wanted to give us two weeks, but I didn't check that we'd arrived at the right time. Did you?"

"No. I seem to remember someone telling me there was no point in checking anything and hurrying me along."

Carrie swallowed. "Sorry. But, if they did make a mistake, that would explain what we're seeing now."

"You mean this could be correct? But our

task's impossible then. We'll never do it. We won't have time before they cut off our only route back."

It seemed hopeless. "I don't know what to say. Without the gateway device we aren't going back anyway. What else can we do? We have to try."

The briefing tablet fell from Dave's hands. He passed a hand over his eyes. The tablet lay on the hot sand, figures blinking on the display, showing the time they had left. *8 hours*, the device read. Eight hours to prevent the placktoids from destroying the future.

CHAPTER SIXTEEN – OVER TO THE DARK SIDE

"I'm not so sure this is a good idea anymore," said Dave as they slipped back inside the mountain. "I mean, we were only just turfed out of here. Maybe we should try somewhere else."

"This has to be our best bet. You said yourself that Harriet might be a clue to something. She's probably still here. And the placktoids must think this is where the Liberator might be. That's why their High Commander's here. So this is where we have to look, too."

"But the placktoids are also looking for *us*."

"And the Liberator. We're in a race to find it now." Carrie paused and adjusted the strap of her bag from over one shoulder to across her chest. They were moving quietly down an empty tunnel and speaking softly. Neither Carrie nor Dave knew exactly what it was that attracted the silver machines and triggered their eviction response, but it was clear that once they identified something as broken or foreign they tried to remove it or seal it away. The two humans couldn't take any chances that the sound of their footsteps or voices would give them away.

Carrie hoped they would find Harriet. She didn't agree with Dave's idea that the robot might have been affected by the Liberator, but if she'd helped them once she might do the same again, and they needed all the allies they could get in this place.

They went silently deeper into the mountain. Time was of the essence. The mountain was huge and they could never search it in eight hours, but they had to try. And that would mean going right to the wire on their deadline to activate the gateway to the future. They walked as quickly as they could. After twenty minutes or so, however, Carrie was compelled to stop. She tugged on her friend's arm and they paused. "Have you noticed something?" she whispered.

"I was just thinking the same thing," Dave replied softly. "Where are all the robots?"

There hadn't been a sign of one in all the time they had been walking.

"And look at that," said Carrie, pointing to a fan in a side tunnel. Its blades were hanging awry and it had stopped turning. The air in the mountain seemed thicker and warmer than before. She wondered how many more fans were broken and waiting to be fixed. "Do you think the placktoids destroyed all of them?"

"I hope not. I'd rather be thrown down the mountain again than meet another placktoid."

They went on, following the twists and turns, going deeper and deeper, away from the upper regions the placktoids had occupied. Carrie's curiosity about the place was piqued. It reminded her of something but she couldn't put her finger on it. As well as the tunnels and fans and liquid streaming through the walls, they passed vast caverns with walls spongy enough to sink a hand into and other areas riddled with small holes. As in the chamber where the High Commander sat, there were sections where the sound of the rushing liquid was loud, sometimes so loud they had to cover their ears.

Carrie would have loved to spend more time investigating the odd place. Gavin hadn't mentioned anything about the strange mountains when he had told them about the planet, and in the hologram they had looked quite ordinary. What had the archaeologists found when they had investigated the placktoid planet? Had they even gone deep below the surface of the mountains?

"Watch out," hissed Dave. They were about to emerge from a tunnel into another, but he forced her back. They huddled against the wall and peeked out. Finally, there were some silver robots. They were gliding in group, heading towards Carrie and Dave. Instead of their usual random formation, however, these robots were flying in a regular pattern, equidistant from each other.

They were heading towards Carrie and Dave's tunnel. As they drew nearer, Carrie and Dave backed away. There was nowhere to hide. "Run," whispered Carrie, and the two sped off in the direction they had come. With luck, the robots wouldn't spot them, and wouldn't take the turn that led them to the humans.

Carrie and Dave were not lucky. Carrie glanced over her shoulder to see the leading robot of the formation take the turn. "Damn, they're after us." She had eaten and drunk and was well rested. She sped away from the approaching robots, hoping that if she put enough distance between them they would lose interest and give up the chase. Glancing over her shoulder again, however, she saw that Dave was already starting to lag.

"Come on," she called.

"My side's killing me," panted Dave. "I landed on it when I got thrown out."

Damn. Carrie eased up a little, but the robots were gaining on them. "Run through the pain," she shouted. "You don't want to get thrown out again."

But Dave's face was twisted into a grimace. He hadn't said anything about being hurt. He'd been underplaying how much the fall from the mountain had affected him. She remembered laughing at him and winced with guilt.

"You go," gasped Dave. "I can't keep up. Better they only catch one of us."

"I'm not leaving you."

"This isn't about you and me, Carrie. We've got a job to do, and one of us has to be able to do it. Run, or they'll get you. It's okay. They're only going to throw me out again. You go ahead. I'll stop and let them pick me up. You keep out of sight and follow, then come to me if you can. If you can't, just go on."

It hurt Carrie to admit it, but he was right. It was hopeless. He would never outrun them, and she couldn't help him. If he got hurt, maybe she could put him somewhere safe while she continued to search for the Liberator. She raced ahead. In a few moments, she heard Dave's shout as he was caught. She grimaced. A narrow side tunnel was just in front of her, so she slipped down it and waited, checking around for more robots. When they passed her, she would follow Dave and the robots that had captured him.

Seconds ticked by. There was no sign of Dave or the robots. Carrie poked her head out of her hiding place for a better look. All around her was empty and silent. Looking around cautiously, she left her hiding place and returned the way she had come. She half walked, half ran for several minutes without sight nor sound of her friend. She was sure she was going the right way. It all looked familiar. Yet Dave and the robots seemed to have vanished.

She sped up her pace further, following the passages that led deeper into the mountain. Were the robots taking a different route to the surface, or were they lost? A horrifying thought struck. Did they have a different plan to dispose of Dave?

Carrie began to sprint. The tunnel walls flew past. How long had she waited for Dave to appear, carried by robots? How long had they been travelling away from her? Only a minute or two, she thought, but the robots glided quickly. Quick enough to catch a running human. She cursed herself for waiting so long.

After racing around a bend in the tunnel, she slid to a halt, barely avoiding plunging into a cavern. It sank into darkness above and below. Around the edge was a narrow path Carrie and Dave had skirted carefully only fifteen or twenty minutes earlier. On the far side were two robots carrying Dave's struggling legs. The last two in the formation that had captured him. She wanted to shout and tell him she was coming, but she didn't dare attract the attention of the robots. She pursed her lips and flew round the cavern's edge, paying barely enough attention to prevent her from plummeting into its depths.

As she reached the other side and the exit Dave had disappeared through, voices murmured in her mind. Her translator was picking up some form of speech. Her heart sank at the sound. It was the voice of the placktoid High Commander.

The robots hadn't taken Dave to dispose of him, they had taken him to the placktoids.

Carrie stopped and bent over, holding her sides while she caught her breath. Her brow wrinkled. The robots had tried to get the placktoids to leave the mountain. Why were they helping them now? Then she remembered the High Commander creating robots of its own. Of course. Neither she nor Dave had seen a difference between the machine the High Commander made and the robots of the mountain, except for a malformation. If the High Commander had perfected the replication process, the robots that had captured Dave belonged to the placktoids. How many had the High Commander made? Had the placktoids destroyed all the original robots and taken over the mountain, filling it with their own?

Carrie slumped to the floor. She rested the back of her head against the wall. She didn't know what to do. Her friend was back in the clutches of the placktoids, but she had a mission to fulfil, to save the future of the galaxy.

CHAPTER SEVENTEEN – CARRIE'S CHOICE

Ten minutes later, Carrie was in the same spot. She was sitting on the tunnel floor with her arms wrapped around her knees, frozen in indecision. She was sure the right thing to do was to abandon her friend and search for the Liberator. What was one life against the trillions that existed across the galaxy of the future? But Dave was her best friend. He'd helped her so much. She might not be around if it weren't for him.

Dave had been the one who'd made her realise her habit of making impulsive, reckless decisions put herself and others in danger. And she didn't want to go back to her old ways and follow what her heart told her without thinking things through. She was trying to follow her friend's advice. But she'd thought this through until her head ached, and all she wanted to do was to try to rescue Dave. All those trillions of lives were in the future. His life was here and now.

She grimaced as she remembered the placktoid High Commander's threat of torture. Was that still its intent? Had it already started? Tears sprang to her eyes. It was no good. Sometimes you just couldn't do the sensible thing. She couldn't give up on Dave, no matter how much she tried to argue herself into it.

Her decision made, Carrie stood and turned, only to bump into a hovering robot that must have come up behind her silently while she was thinking. She backed away, imagining it was about to grab her, but then she paused. This robot was alone. Normally they travelled in groups—organised groups under the placktoids' instruction. And it wasn't doing anything. It wasn't trying to grab her and remove her, or fixing something. It was only hovering, expectantly it seemed.

Carrie's eyes grew wide and she sank to her knees, placing her hands on the front of the robot. "Harriet," she breathed, "you found me."

Now that Carrie had finally figured out who it was, Harriet did a strange thing. She popped her lid. The whole upper half opened, rotating on a hinge on one of her longest sides, so that she looked like an open, lozenge-shaped book. Carrie had only seen the robots open their underbellies before. She leaned over to peer inside, and gasped. The upper half of Harriet, which slotted over her central tool mechanism, was empty. In the lower half Carrie could see the folded and slotted tools from above, but nestled in a space to one side was Dave's Liaison Officer equipment bag. Somehow, Harriet had found it and brought it to her.

"Oh, thank you, thank you," Carrie exclaimed as she lifted out the bag. Pulling it open, she checked for the single most important thing it could contain, and exhaled loudly when she saw it: the gateway-opening device. It was still there. All was not lost. If she could rescue Dave and they could find the Liberator before the deadline, they could go home.

Carrie quickly slung Dave's bag over her head and other shoulder so that the two straps crossed over her chest. "Harriet, was it you who gave me my bag back as well? I don't know why or how you're helping us, but I can't thank you enough. We owe you our lives. But I have to go now. I have to rescue Dave."

The robot didn't react or respond to Carrie's words. It hovered with its top half open.

Now that Carrie had made her decision—for better or worse—and she had the gateway device, she was determined to leave right away. With grim satisfaction she realised she now had Dave's weapons as well as her own. But she wondered why Harriet didn't go now that she'd given over Dave's bag.

Carrie reached over and closed the robot's lid, but it sprang open again. Whatever locking device it had, Harriet wasn't activating it. Carrie gave up. "I'm sorry, I have to go. I have to help my friend."

She turned to leave, but the robot bumped her. She turned back. "What do you want?" Carrie asked, her hands on her hips.

The robot lowered itself until it was hovering just above the ground. Carrie tilted her head. What was Harriet trying to tell her? The robot waggled, bumping her upper lid against the floor. Carrie frowned and studied the machine's interior again. Did she have something else she wanted to give her?

The area around the central box, where Harriet had stowed Dave's bag, was surprisingly roomy. Was it a crumple zone to protect the tools if the robot was in an accident? She rubbed her chin. Surprisingly roomy. Was it big enough for her to fit? It would be a squeeze, but if she curled around the box... "Do you want me to get inside you?"

Harriet still didn't reply. There was only one way to find out. Carrie lifted her Liaison Officer equipment bags and tucked them into the recess on one side of the robot's tool store, then lowered herself into the other side. The robot took the additional weight easily, rising a little higher.

Carrie waited. Now was the acid test. Would Harriet eject her? Or if she'd wanted Carrie to climb in she would...The lid swung up and over. It closed with a click, sealing Carrie in. That was it. She had placed her fate in an anonymous machine's hands...or whatever.

Her stomach fell as Harriet rose and glided away. As far as Carrie could tell, the robot was heading towards the area the copies of her kind had taken Dave. For better or worse, they were heading to the placktoids.

***

Carrie quickly became uncomfortable cramped within Harriet's shell. The close confinement was completely dark and stuffy, but she had no choice but to remain there until Harriet let her out—hopefully soon. As she was carried along Carrie tried to guess why Harriet had wanted to get in. Presumably it was to hide her from the placktoids. She must have known Carrie would never get through to Dave without being spotted. Now that they had the silver robots working for them, Harriet could slip in unnoticed. She was identical to the rest. It was only her behaviour that set her apart, so if she acted the same as the other robots, the placktoids would never guess she had a stowaway.

What would she do if Harriet managed to get her to Dave? Carrie didn't have a plan. Even if Dave was alone, she didn't know how she would get him out. Harriet was barely large enough to hold her. Dave would never fit in as well. If there were some robots left who weren't made by the placktoids, maybe Harriet could persuade one of them to carry Dave, but she doubted he would fit. She sighed. She would have to cross that bridge when she came to it.

Another question that bothered her was about Harriet herself. Why was she so different from the other robots? The rest were like automatons, incapable of independent thought and much less intelligent than their descendants, the placktoids. What had happened to Harriet to make her different? Had she been affected by the Liberator as Dave thought? Or had the Creators deliberately made her different? But why? Or was she the result of an automated production process operating over thousands of years without being checked or calibrated? The

Creators seemed to have departed the planet, leaving their robots behind. The machines must have been programmed to create new individuals to replace those that broke or reached the end of their pre-determined lifespan. When robots were replacing themselves, had the process become corrupted, the information subtly altering, like a photocopy of a photocopy of a photocopy? Had Harriet appeared like a random mutation in some weird facsimile of biological evolution?

Harriet stopped, and her lid opened. Carrie was flooded with welcome air. She lifted her head and peeked over the side. They were alone in a small, dim chamber, similar to the place where the placktoids had put her and Dave when they gave them the truth drug. Gripping the side of the robot, Carrie got out. She retrieved the two Liaison Officer toolkits and passed the straps over her head. She was determined not to become separated from either of them again.

Patting both bags, Carrie scanned the empty chamber. Why had Harriet brought her here? Was this where the placktoids would bring Dave soon? From outside came the grinding, trundling sounds of the evil mechanical aliens moving about. They were close by. Harriet had got her through their lines unnoticed, but now it was up to her to try to find her friend.

But as Carrie stepped across the chamber on her way to the entrance she caught her foot and tripped, falling flat on her face. Sitting up, she rubbed her nose. She turned to see what had tripped her, and her heart stopped. There was a raised bump on the floor. It was the same colour, which had made it hard to see. A coffin-sized bump. A bump the size of Dave.

The robots had entombed him.

Carrie immediately hit the surface, trying to break through the skin. But though the material was thin, it was tough, and her blows left no mark. She tried kicking the bump instead, with similar effect. Should she fire a weapon at the material? But that would probably kill Dave. She riffled through her equipment bag. She had nothing that might help.

Harriet closed her lid with a click. She seemed to be waiting.

"Harriet, my friend's trapped again. Can you get him out like you did when you helped us before? Please open it up."

The silver robot didn't react. Carrie pushed her towards the bump. "Please, get Dave out."

As if in reply, the robot's underbelly opened and her tool cache lowered. But no tool appeared. Carrie peered at the machine's undercarriage. In the container of tools that folded neatly away into its belly, there was an empty slot. One seemed to be missing. Harriet didn't have the tool that would open Dave's tomb.

CHAPTER EIGHTEEN – DROP OUTS

Thumping her hand on the surface of the lump, Carrie almost called Dave's name but stopped herself just in time. There was no point in getting her friend out if she attracted the attention of the placktoids. The wall of her friend's tomb was like fibreglass. Her fist didn't even make an impression. The only result of hitting the bump was a sore hand.

Carrie bent down and put her ear to the surface. No sound came from within. No shouting or calling. Not even a returning thump. Was the material soundproof? Or was Dave not responding because he didn't realise it was her, or was he unconscious already? Panic seized Carrie and she hit the lump again. She winced and put her hand under her armpit. "We've got to do something, Harriet. He doesn't have much air in there. He could've run out of oxygen already."

Harriet's response was immediate. She glided around the bump to the other side.

"You understand me, don't you?" said Carrie. "Have you learned English through listening to me and Dave? Or did you scan our brains?" She shook her head. "If only you could answer me."

The robot had paused at end of the tomb farthest from Carrie. She bobbed up and down a few times as if trying to show her something. "What is it, Harriet?" Carrie joined the robot on the other side. As she arrived at the spot she gasped. A man-sized hole opened in the tomb there, surrounded by fragments of the wall. Bending down, she peered in. Inside was nothing but shadowy darkness.

Dave had escaped.

Carrie's heart leaped. Somehow, her friend had managed to break through the wall and get out. But where was he? Now she had to find both him *and* the Liberator before their time was up. About to leave, she paused to pick up a fragment of the material that had sealed Dave in. How had he got out? He didn't have anything with him that he could cut it with. Or did he? She looked at Harriet. Suddenly some things started to make sense.

"Harriet, can you help me again? I need to find Dave, but if I go out there the placktoids will see me." The robot's lid popped open. Carrie deposited her bags and climbed inside. Harriet's motion was smooth as she glided away.

In a few moments they were once more in among the placktoids. The noise of their various methods of locomotion reverberated in Carrie's narrow hiding place. She thought the placktoids had come down a notch since the days of their predecessors. Harriet's smooth, noiseless motion was far better. Even the gliding placktoids, such as the ones that resembled paperclips, vibrated loudly and put her teeth on edge.

The placktoids probably thought themselves superior to their ancestors, the homogeneous, comparatively simple robots that maintained the mountain interiors, but in Carrie's opinion the silver robots were the best. They didn't capture and destroy other species, and they didn't want to rule the galaxy.

The noise of the placktoids grew quieter, and in a short time Harriet stopped. Carrie happily got ready to emerge from confinement, but Harriet's lid remained closed. Carrie squirmed and pushed upward, but it was shut tight. She stopped pushing and tried to relax, thinking that maybe it wasn't safe for her to get out just yet. Maybe there were placktoids or corrupted robots nearby.

She tried to be patient, but inside Harriet's shell the temperature was rising. Carrie wondered if the robot had stopped in a patch of sunlight. Carrie squirmed some more. She was wet with sweat and feeling light-headed. If Harriet didn't open up soon she thought she might faint.

At last the lid swung open and daylight streamed in. Carrie had been right. The were in full sunlight. If Harriet hadn't let her out soon she would have been cooked. She would have to explain to the robot and ask her not to do that in the future.

Raising her head cautiously above the edge of Harriet's shell, Carrie peeked out. A hot wind ruffled her hair. On one side lay the opening to a dim, shadowy tunnel, on the other, empty air. They were high up. Below them the mountainside stretched several hundred metres in a sheer drop. Her stomach clenched at the thought of what would have happened if she had leapt out without looking. But why had Harriet brought her here? Where was Dave? She looked again into the tunnel. It was empty, though presumably minutes ago something threatening had been there.

Through the whistle of the wind came a small sound. Something like a gasp. The noise came from below Harriet. Carrie sat up a little more, clutching the sides of the shell as the robot wobbled in response to her movement. Peering over the side, Carrie had to stop herself from crying out. Just below, clinging to the edge of the tunnel with his fingertips, dangling above the fatal drop, was her friend.

"Dave," she hissed, hoping the surprise of hearing her voice wouldn't make him let go. He didn't respond, though his eyes grew round. "Dave."

"C-Carrie?" he whispered, squinting upward at Harriet.

"Yes, it's me. I'm right above you. Can't you see?"

"I can hardly see anything. I'm looking right into a sun."

"I'm in Harriet. What are you doing?"

"What do think I'm doing? I'm hiding from the

—ahhh," he exclaimed as one of his hands lost its grip. He swung for a second before managing to grab hold of the lip of the tunnel again. "I-I can't hold on much longer."

"Harriet," said Carrie, "quick, go under—" She gulped. Placktoids had appeared at the end of the tunnel, and they were heading straight for them. Carrie reached for her bag, her heart lurching as Harriet wobbled again. She fumbled for her weapon. The placktoids were nearly upon them before her hand closed gratefully around it. Pulling it out, she fired. The beam sliced through the leading placktoids' armour, leaving a smoking trail. The acrid stench of burning filled the air. As the placktoids in front halted, the ones coming from behind ran into them.

"Carrie," called Dave, "I can't..." He grunted with effort.

"Just a little longer." Carrie fired again as the still-mobile placktoids pushed the ones blocking them aside. The laser seared into the new assailants, sending more acrid smoke billowing. Strangely, the placktoids didn't return fire, even though Carrie was a sitting duck in Harriet. But, whatever the reason, she was grateful for it. If she could just destroy the placktoids in the tunnel, she could save her friend and they could escape.

The third wave of placktoids surged over the blackened remains of their comrades.

"Carrie," yelled Dave.

She blasted the mechanical aliens apart. That was the last of them. But at the end of the tunnel more appeared. Carrie's heart sank.

"Ahhhhh..."

Her gaze flew to Dave. He had finally lost his grip and was in free fall down the side of the mountain.

"Harriet," screamed Carrie, "save him."

With a terrifying lurch, the machine sank through the air. Carrie held on with white knuckles as Harriet tipped and her speed of descent increased. "Dave, we're coming," Carrie called, but the hot wind whipped her words from her mouth.

The wind whistled in her ears and the mountain became a blur as they dropped faster and faster. Below them an outcrop loomed. Carrie couldn't breathe. Would they save her friend before he hit it?

They passed him, spreadeagled, his mouth open and gaping. Then they were under him and travelling at nearly the same speed. Carrie grabbed Dave's legs as Harriet slowed a little more. His boot was in Carrie's face. She pushed it away and tried to guide her friend over Harriet's open shell. Harriet slowed further and more of Dave was safely over Harriet, but the ground was approaching at a dizzyingly fast pace.

"Stop wriggling," said Carrie as her friend struggled and turned in the air.

Harriet lurched. Dave bumped his head on the edge of her shell. He reached round and gripped it. Looking down, Carrie realised that though

Harriet had slowed a lot the robot would never stop in time. She squeezed her eyes shut and sank her fingers into her friend's legs as they hit the slope at the foot of the mountain. There was a whirling blur of hot sand, rocks and scree as the three tumbled down the mountain. Carrie caught a brief glimpse of Dave sliding to a halt. Harriet's open lid caught on a boulder and bent, stopping her dead. Carrie broke loose. She felt a sharp pain in her head and saw sparks, then nothing.

CHAPTER NINETEEN – LIGHT IN THE DARK

"Carrie, Carrie."

As she opened her eyes Carrie found herself looking into Dave's anxious face.

"What a relief," he said. "I thought you'd never wake up."

She was flat on her back on the sand in the shade of a boulder. She lifted herself onto her elbows and winced as a pain lanced through her head. "What happened? Is Harriet okay?" She tried to sit up, but everything started to turn black. She grimaced and lay down.

"You hit your head. You were out cold. The placktoids started shooting at us, so I dragged you here. We're not safe. We have to move. I can see some sort of opening in the ground close by. If we can make it there maybe we can get away."

"What about Harriet?"

"I don't think she made it. Her lid is open and her tools are scattered everywhere. Can you move?"

Carrie sat up again, ignoring the pain that spread across her skull. "Yes, but we have to save Harriet."

"We can't, Carrie. How can we? Anyway, she's fine. The placktoids don't want her. They were firing at us."

"She isn't fine if she's all twisted and broken. If we don't take her with us, the scavengers will come and dismantle her to use her parts for other robots."

"Carrie, it's only a robot."

"She isn't only a robot. She saved your life. She saved both our lives. She isn't like the others." Wincing, Carrie lifted herself to a crouch and peered round the boulder. She caught a quick glimpse of the broken remains of Harriet a few metres away. Far above, placktoids were emerging from the tunnel entrance in the side of the mountain. "Come on. I'm sure between us we can carry her. I bet she isn't that heavy."

"Carrie," hissed Dave as she ran out from the cover of the rock. A second later he followed. "I can't believe we're doing this."

A laser beam hit the ground as Carrie reached the side of the stricken robot. Dave was right. Harriet was a mess. Her shell was dented and scraped and her lid was partially detached. The two Liaison Officer bags had survived the fall, tucked into her recesses. Harriet's tools were scattered about, but Dave was scooping them up and pushing them into the front of his jumpsuit, which reminded Carrie of a bone she had to pick with him. But that would have to wait.

The sand sizzled and melted in a patch next to her friend, sending a shock of fear through

Carrie. "Quick," she shouted, grabbing one end of Harriet's shell. Dave grabbed the other end, and they ran, crouching, towards the hole Dave had seen. More laser strikes hit the ground around them. Carrie wondered at the placktoids' inaccuracy. They were high tech. It should have been easy for them to blast her and Dave to frizzled, charred lumps. She shivered and shook the image from her mind. They were nearly at the hole. It was a crack that opened in the rocky ground, barely large enough for them to fit through. There was no time to check what was inside. They would have to take their chances.

Carrying the disabled robot between them, Carrie and Dave leapt into blackness. Empty space opened out below them and, silently, the three fell. Carrie's stomach lurched. There seemed to be no bottom to the hole, or at least no bottom near enough that there wouldn't be a serious impact when they hit. She couldn't hold on to the robot. Harriet left her hands and went sailing and spinning in the air, glinting in the sunlight that beamed from above.

Carrie briefly noticed something shimmering below before she hit it and sank like a stone. It wasn't water. It tasted sour and salty. It was the liquid that flowed through the mountain. Except this was a lake of it, or rather a river, for the current tugged at her. She kicked, trying to rise against its pull. She remembered with gratitude teaching Dave to swim only a few weeks before. If she hadn't he wouldn't have stood a chance. But what about Harriet? Would she fall to the bottom, the weight of her metal dragging her down? Or was her propulsion system still working well enough to take her to safety?

Air was forcing itself from Carrie's lungs. Where was the surface of the liquid? Surely she must have risen enough now. But what if there was no gap between the river and the roof of the tunnel? What if there was only rock and no air for her to breathe?

Carrie smashed into a rocky wall and bubbles were forced from her lips. With all her strength she fought the instinct to breathe in. Though her eyes were open she could see only blackness. Had she got disoriented? Was she swimming down or sideways instead of up? Her lungs were screaming at her to breathe in. Blood pulsed in her ears.

Then there was air. Chill air on her wet face. Carrie breathed in with a great whoop, then out, then in again. As she caught her breath she trod water. Despite the total darkness she could feel herself being carried along. In the pitch black there was nothing she could do but allow the river to take her where it would, hoping that Dave and Harriet were being swept in the same direction. Dave. "Dave?" she called.

"Carrie? "Where are you? Are you in the river?"

"Yes, where are you?"

"I'm on a bank. Over here. Follow my voice."

He seemed to be behind her. Carrie turned and began swimming upstream. "Where are you, Dave? I can't see a thing."

"This way. Keep swimming. There's a bank on the edge of the river. I brushed up against it."

The pull of the current was strong. Carrie wasn't sure she was making any headway. She could even have been moving away from her friend. She worked her arms and legs harder, pulling through the water. "Keep talking."

"This way. Over here. Keeping going, Carrie. You can make it."

His voice sounded closer. Her fingertips brushed something solid. Sand. She kicked and pulled with her arms. More sand. A solid bottom. A few seconds later she was out of the water. She collapsed, gasping, on the wet sandy shore.

She heard shuffling and a hand grabbed her arm. "You did it," said Dave. "Quick, come this way. Away from the edge." He tugged on her arms and she scrambled and crawled up the sand to where it was dry.

After catching her breath a little, Carrie said, "Is Harriet here? Did she find her way out too?"

"I don't think so," came Dave's voice from beside her. "I'll check." The sand rustled as he crawled away. A minute later, "I found her. Or I think so. Unless it's another robot that got beached here."

"There's an easy way to find out. Feel around inside her. If we're lucky, our bags will still be wedged in there."

"Did you say bags? Both of them?"

"Yes. Harriet found them and brought them to me."

"You're kidding."

"Have a look. Or a feel. I mean."

Silence. The rustle of wet cloth. A gasp of exclamation from Dave. The clink and chink of metal and plastic devices. "Where is it?" muttered Dave. More scraping and rustling. "Is this it? Yes." A click and a beam of light, which turned to Carrie.

She held her hand before her eyes. "Point that away. You're blinding me."

"I'll be damned. We got our equipment back. Hang on a sec, I'll bring you your bag."

A few moments later her friend was beside her and pushing her bag into her hands. In the light from his torch Carrie searched through it and found her own torch. She turned it on and pointed it at Dave, though angled away from his eyes. He was scraped, bruised and wet, and his uniform was torn. Carrie imagined she must look much the same. "Well, we're still alive."

"Only just," replied Dave. "The placktoids must have seen where we went. I wonder how long it'll take them to find us down here?"

"How much longer have we got?"

Dave pulled the briefing device from his bag. "Not long."

"How long?"

"Three hours."

CHAPTER TWENTY – HARRIET UNVEILED

A short time later, Carrie and Dave were slumped on the ground in the same spot. With the help of their torches, they'd searched the river bank. There was no escape. The bank they'd landed on was only a few metres wide and deep. Behind them the rocky wall was solid and stretched smoothly to the roof of the cave without any foot- or handholds, let alone any exit. Before them the turbulent river ran, glinting blue in the torchlight.

"Any ideas?" asked Dave.

Carrie shrugged. "Swim? Maybe there's an exit to the surface further down, or maybe the river flows under a mountain into a cave where we can get out."

"I don't like the sound of that. You know I'm still not a very strong swimmer, and who knows where this river goes? What if it flows into a tunnel with no air space where we can breathe? Or the liquid gets sucked up into those channels that run through the mountains. No, if we swim we'll probably drown."

"Well, we've got to do something, and

quickly."

"I've got an idea." His head dropped a little, lengthening the shadow it cast on the wall behind him in the light of Carrie's torch. "I don't think you'll like it though." He looked away as he continued, "The way I see it, we've done all we can. We've tried our best, but we haven't managed to find the Liberator, and there are far too many placktoids for us to defeat them all. The whole population has come here from the future. They must be in every mountain."

Carrie didn't like the sound of where this speech seemed to be heading.

"We're stuck here. Trying to get out is almost certain death, and no one's going to benefit from us dying. But there is one way out. And we've got more than two and a half hours to take it."

"No."

He sighed. "I thought you'd say that. But what choice do we have? We have to give up and open the gateway back to our time."

"We were sent here to do a job. Everyone in the future is depending on us. We can't just give up and chicken out."

"It isn't chickening out. I'm just trying to be realistic."

"No, you aren't. You're imagining the worst like you always do."

"And I'm always right."

Carrie stood up, her lips tight. "Not this time you aren't. Not this time." She went to where

Harriet was lying at the edge of the river. The robot hadn't moved all the time they'd been there. It seemed as though she had dragged herself to the bank with the last of her energy and was now irretrievably broken. Carrie held out her hand. "Give me her tools."

"Why? What are you going to do?"

"I'm going to put them back inside her."

"What's the point?"

Carrie let out a gasp of frustration. "Just give them to me. Does everything I do have to have a reason? I want to put her back together, that's all. Maybe it'll make a difference. I don't know. And give me the one you stole too."

Dave had begun to gather the robot's tools from the sand. He'd taken them out of his jumpsuit when he'd got to shore. He paused as he picked up one. "Huh?"

"Don't act all innocent. I figured out how you got out when the robots sealed you in a tomb again. You stole from Harriet the tool that can break through the material, didn't you? When you were examining her and I fell asleep. That's why she went off, isn't it?"

Dave sighed. "I didn't think it mattered. I thought it would come in useful in case we got sealed in again." He placed a handful of tools on the sand next to Carrie. "And when the robot left I couldn't stop her and replace the tool."

Carrie tutted.

"But it worked out in the end," Dave went on. "I might have run out of oxygen by the time you got to me."

"Hmpf. If Harriet hadn't gone and left us you might not have been captured in the first place. We're lucky she decided to help us anyway and went and got our bags back from under the placktoids' noses." She was trying to match the tools to their corresponding slots in Harriet's central mechanism. After several tries, she finally found one that seemed to fit. She slotted it in place. "Bingo." She picked up another tool.

Dave knelt next to her and angled his torch to give Carrie more light. "I don't know. It's strange, isn't it? This robot..." Carrie gave him a look. "...Harriet, I mean. Why does she behave differently from the rest? She's helped us escape from the placktoids twice now. She got us our equipment back. What's made her do it all?"

"I've been wondering about that too. I think she's developed a kind of moral code. We saw what the placktoids did to the other robots, and they've probably been doing the same all over the planet. Those robots are Harriet's...I don't know...friends and relations? We haven't harmed a single one. I think she's decided we're the goodies, and she wants to be on our side. Maybe she hopes we can stop what the placktoids are doing."

"You keep talking about her as if she's still working."

"There you go again." Carrie rolled her eyes as she stubbornly slotted another tool into place.

"But why was, or is, she even like that?"

"I'm not sure, but I think it's a kind of evolution. The Creators, whoever they were, have been gone for millenia from the look of things, leaving these robots to look after the mountains. Goodness knows why. Somewhere there must be a place where the robots can replicate themselves or they would have all worn out and broken down by now. Gavin told us they had a fixed lifespan, so they need replacements. But they've been replacing themselves for so long, there must be errors in transmission of the construction blueprint from one generation to the next, like mutations in genetic code. My guess is that Harriet here is a mistake. Something went wrong when she was made, and whatever the mistake was it's given her the ability to learn and behave independently.

"She's learned English from listening to us. I'm sure of it. I think she must have heard me saying we needed food and water. Maybe she didn't know what food and water was, but she'd seen the placktoids take our bags—yours from the tunnel when you dropped it, and mine when we were captured—and she guessed that there was something we needed from them. So, despite the fact that you stole one of her tools..." Carrie paused as she was fitting a tool and glared at Dave "...she went and got them for us."

"It's an interesting idea. And her behaviour does bear it out, I have to admit. Shame it had to end here really, isn't it? If she could have passed on her advantages so all the robots had them, they might have stood a chance against the placktoids."

"Yeah." Carrie couldn't find the right spot for the tool she was holding. She tossed it down on the sand and rested her arms on Harriet's shell. "I hope she isn't dead. Hey, if we can get her going again, maybe we can explain that's what she needs to do, and we can send her off to do that. Then we can think about going back to our time. It would be something."

"Hmm. If she can pass on her knowledge and abilities to the other robots—" Dave gaped. He breathed in so sharply he made a whooping noise and he stared, wide-eyed at the lifeless robot. "If she can pass on her abilities to the other robots, it means she must be..."

"What? What do you..." The penny dropped, and Carrie leapt to her feet and stumbled backwards into the shallows of the river. "No, it can't be. It can't be. She doesn't look anything like that machine we saw in the placktoid creation story. No, no, no. Not Harriet." She stared at the robot's bent shell and half-complete tool mechanism. Her face was stricken as she turned her gaze to her friend.

She fell to her knees, barely feeling the cool liquid that soaked through the trousers of her jumpsuit. Her eyes brimmed with tears. "We can't do it."

"I'm sorry, Carrie, but we have to. It has to be her. She's unique among the rest of them. And this isn't only about a robot that's helped us. The entire future of the galaxy is at stake."

"But we don't know for sure."

"You're right. We don't. But we can't afford to

take a chance either." He put a hand on her arm. "Carrie, it's only a machine."

She threw off his hand and leapt to her feet. "No," she shouted, even though what Dave had guessed made sense. It explained so much, not least why the placktoids hadn't been able to find Harriet at first. Over the centuries their image of their great saviour had changed, taking on epic proportions. They hadn't been expecting to find a small, nondescript robot identical to the rest.

"I don't care if she is the Liberator. I'm not going to let you kill her."

CHAPTER TWENTY-ONE – BATTLE OF THE BUDDIES

Dave wouldn't destroy Harriet without her agreement, Carrie didn't think, at least not until the last minute, when they had to choose between returning to their own time or living out a miserable, short existence on an alien planet thousands of years in the past. But for the last half hour he'd been wearing her down with rational, logical arguments, and he wouldn't stop until she gave in. She had no sensible reply to his statements.

"But it isn't certain she's the Liberator," she said, continuing to play for time, hoping a reason for sparing Harriet would pop into her head.

Dave rubbed his neck, sending exaggerated shadows sliding over the rock face behind him. "We've been over this so many times. It adds up. She's different from the other robots, and she wants to help them. She must want to save them from their inevitable deaths too. And it explains why the placktoids didn't hit us with their lasers when we were with her. They've finally realised she's the Liberator and they didn't want to risk damaging her. They must think she's still important in their plan to hasten the development of autonomous, thinking robots."

"But she doesn't look anything like—"

"Carrie, creatures from mythology frequently don't look anything like the things that inspired them. You're too smart not to know that, as I've already said." His tone was strained.

"But what if, what if..." The germ of an idea was forming. She frowned as she tried to grasp it. "What if Harriet had nothing to do with giving the placktoids immortality? We've seen how they're bending them to their cause. The High Commander is manufacturing new ones. What if the change was nothing to do with the Liberator? Maybe it's a weird time loop thing. You know, like they're their own grandfathers."

"What?"

"It's a well known time theory. It says time already exists from the beginning to the end, and we can't change anything. It's already set."

"Then what are we doing here? We can't change anything."

"Us deciding to come here is part of it. We don't really get to choose, or we think we do, but the choice is inevitable."

"What?"

"Never mind. The point is, the placktoids of the future might have been the cause of the change in the placktoids of the past."

"But then why wouldn't their history show that? Why have they created a mythology showing something entirely different?"

"Because it was so long ago," Carrie replied.

"Stories change over time, and don't forget that the placktoids have culture. It isn't like they're transmitting data from one generation to the next. The information's been affected by their beliefs, attitudes, values and so on."

Dave's eyes narrowed. "You're leading me down a rabbit hole, aren't you? Whatever you say, it doesn't matter. We have to destroy the robot to be on the safe side."

Harriet was lying on the sand next to the arguing friends. She twitched. She lifted a centimetre off the sand and dropped down again. Her lid moved, as if she were trying to close it.

No, not now, thought Carrie. *Please.* Harriet twitched again. Her lid lifted and dropped and rose again. It closed but the seal wasn't complete. The metal was too bent out of shape.

They looked at each other in silence. "I'm sorry, Carrie," Dave said. "We're running out of time. I don't have a choice." He stood and went towards his bag, which was lying open on the sand. His intent was clear. He didn't make it far. Carrie threw herself at him and flung her arms around his thighs, rugby-tackling him. They both landed face downwards with a thump.

"You're not doing it," she exclaimed in a muffled tone. Her face was buried in the back of Dave's legs. She was gripping them like a vice.

"Let me go." He struggled against Carrie's grasp. He kicked and wriggled, but she clung on. "I have to do it." Giving up on Carrie releasing his legs, he began to pull forward on his elbows, dragging her along with him. He inched closer to his bag.

"No," shouted Carrie, jumping up and racing forward. As she passed her friend, he shoved her to one side, sending her into the rocky wall. "Ow," she exclaimed. So he wanted to play rough? She pushed up her sleeves to her elbows.

Dave had reached his bag and was looking inside. Carrie kicked it out of his hands. It flew across the bank and landed perilously close to the water, its contents spilling out.

"Don't be an idiot," yelled Dave. "Our only way home is in there." He ran towards the bag.

Carrie darted forwards and stopped between him and his bag. She took her Bagua Zhang stance. "Even if Harriet is the Liberator, she hasn't done anything yet. She hasn't changed the other robots. They aren't evil like the placktoids. We don't have the right to destroy her when she hasn't done any harm. This plan was wrong-headed from the start. We can't destroy sentient beings because of what they *might* do."

Dave hesitated. His arms dropped to his sides. "Carrie, I can't fight you. You know I can't."

She held her hands steady. "Well you're going to have to try if you want to kill Harriet." Behind her, the robot was slowing regaining power. She hovered a metre or so above the bank.

"What do you want me to do, Carrie? We have to save the galaxy from the placktoids, even if it means destroying the thing that's helped us." Carrie didn't move an inch. Dave gripped his hair and let go. His face became grim. "All right. If that's what you want." He made his hands into fists and held them up in a boxer's stance. He had folded his thumbs inside, next to his palms.

Carrie rolled her eyes. "Come on, then." She would have to be careful not to let him get a punch in or he might break his thumbs. She skipped forward and pushed his hip with the sole of her foot. He stumbled back. Dave made small circles with his fists and lowered his head. Carrie bit her lip to stop herself from smiling.

Her friend jabbed with his right. Carrie ducked under the blow and wrestled him. She hooked a heel behind his leg to unbalance him and held onto him as he fell so that he wouldn't hit the ground too hard. In less than a second she had him pinned down. He struggled a few moments before giving up. He sighed. "That was easy, wasn't it?"

Carrie nodded.

Her friend relaxed on the sand. "So, what are you going to do? Hold me here until the deadline's passed? It won't matter. As soon as I get the chance I'll destroy her. I have to."

He was right. Carrie turned to the hovering, battered robot. "Go, Harriet. Get away. Fly away and don't come back." But the robot didn't move. "Go away, please. Now, or he's going to destroy you. Don't you understand?" Still Harriet made no movement. She seemed to be watching or waiting for something.

"She doesn't get what you're saying. She won't leave, so you might as well give up. You're going to have to release me eventually," said

Dave. "You're going to get thirsty or hungry. You can't hold me here forever."

Damn that robot. Why wouldn't she leave? Before, it had seemed like she could understand what they said. She must know what was going on. So why stay when her life was in danger? Carrie was missing something important like she always did. Like she had at work, when Dave had told her to watch what the managers did, not listen to what they said. But Harriet wasn't doing anything. What did it mean?

She had it. This would make Dave listen. She relaxed her grip on her friend. He immediately wriggled out from under her and went to get his weapon. "Wait, Dave. Please, wait." She put herself between him and the robot and held up her hands.

He pointed the weapon at the ground. "Carrie, I'm sorry, but—"

"You said to take notice of what people do, not what they say, didn't you? Look at her."

She stepped to one side. His gaze went to the hovering robot.

"She knows what we're saying," Carrie went on. "I'm sure of it. I don't know how much she understands about the placktoids and why they're here, but she knows what you're going to do. And she isn't leaving. She could go now, or she could fly at you and knock you into the water, but she isn't. I don't know what she did that made the placktoids evolve as they have, or if she had anything to do with it. But she isn't malicious. She selfless. She understands she might have had something to do with what happened to her species, and she's willing to let you kill her to prevent it. Doesn't that tell you she can't be responsible? Or at least that she'll do everything in her power to prevent it, even losing her own life? How can it be right to destroy her?"

Dave's hand fell to his side. "You're right. I should take my own advice. She can't speak, but her behaviour tells us all we need to know. It would be wrong and stupid to kill her." He slumped down. "Then what do we do?"

"We go after the creatures we know are evil. Like the High Commander. If we get him we can stop him from creating evil robots. Maybe the time loop theory is correct. You never know, when we return to the present, there might be no placktoids, or they might be kind and gentle like Harriet."

Her friend snorted. "Huh, I'd like to see that."

CHAPTER TWENTY-TWO – A SLIPPERY TRIP

Carrie checked the briefing device. They had one hour left before they would have to open the gateway to their time. Sitting opposite her, in Harriet's open lid, Dave was looking nervous.

"Are you sure she can carry us both?" he asked.

"That's the third time you've asked me that and the answer's the same. No, I'm not sure, but it doesn't matter because we'll find out soon enough when she starts to lift off."

Dave didn't look convinced. "What happens if she can carry us for a little way, but then her power gives out and she drops us in the river?"

"Stop worrying, won't you? If we're too heavy for her she won't try it, I'm sure. Now, have we got everything?"

Carrie and Dave had replaced all of Harriet's tools that Dave had managed to retrieve, plus the one he'd stolen. She was still missing a few, but that couldn't be helped. They would just have to hope she or they didn't need the missing tools for the job they had coming up. They had packed up their Liaison Officer toolboxes after checking that the weapons to attack the placktoids were still functional. A segment of blasted, melted rock had given them their answer.

They swept the sand bank with their torches but couldn't see anything they'd left behind. "Okay, time to go," said Carrie.

"Hold on, one more thing we haven't discussed."

"What's that?" Carrie was impatient to be off. They were wasting precious minutes.

"If we don't manage to find them in time, or we can't get close enough to the High Commander to destroy it, we bail, right? Just open the gateway and leave. We've done the best we can in the circumstances to prevent the placktoids from having control of the galaxy in our time. The Council can't expect us to do any more."

"Hmmm...okay. But we should leave it as late as we can. If we can get through our gateway just minutes before they lay down the time shield, the placktoids won't be able to follow us. They'll be trapped here forever, and when we get back to our present they won't exist. They'll be trapped in their own past."

"It's risky, but...okay, agreed. I'm going to look up that word Gavin told us to open the gateway so we don't mess up at the last minute. Woah." Harriet had lurched up, clearly understanding what they were saying and in a hurry to get away. Dave grabbed the side of the upper shell with one hand while he felt inside his bag with the other.

Carrie was crouched in her side of Harriet's shell, which housed the tool mechanism. It was a tight, awkward fit even sitting up, but it made sense for her to sit there and not Dave because she was the smaller of the two. She rubbed Harriet's bent shell affectionately and wondered if she could come through the gateway with them to the future. The thought of leaving her alone in this world of evil placktoids and their mindless, slow-witted ancestors made her sad.

The sentient robot hovered above the sand, as if testing her ability to carry the weight of the two humans, then glided out over the water. Carrie shone her torch ahead, its light glinting on the rough waves of blue liquid. Dave kept his head low and his eyes fixed on his briefing tablet.

After a few minutes' travel, Carrie began to appreciate the experience. The air was pleasantly cool and moist compared to the surface, and she had never been on an underground river before so she enjoyed the novelty. There was little sound but the rushing of the water, which echoed in the close walls of the tunnel. Then she heard a plop.

She didn't quite believe her ears at first because she didn't know of anything that would make such a noise in that world. It sounded nothing like a robot. It was something organic and heavy. Another plop resounded from the water and repeated as it echoed from the walls. She swung her light across the liquid. "Did you hear that?"

"Nope," said Dave in the tone of someone who

had heard something but was choosing to ignore it.

Two more plops followed in close succession. Carrie turned her torch in the direction of the sound but saw nothing but the familiar rippling surface. "Do you think there are things living in that liquid?"

"Do you mean, are there things living in the liquid we were dragged through and nearly drowned in, and have just spent an hour or so sitting right next to? My answer is, there better bloody well not be."

"But it makes sense, doesn't it? The planet surface isn't very hospitable to life, but under here, away from the suns, it would be easier for creatures to live." She put a hand to her mouth and her eyes widened. "Do you think this is where the Creators are?"

"I don't think so. Why would they create robots to keep the mountains empty of rubbish and working? They would make robots to look after them, wouldn't they?"

"Not if the mountains are important to their survival."

Dave shook his head. "Let's just concentrate on the job we've come to do, okay?" At 'okay' there was a large plop right next to Harriet, and the liquid splashed, soaking Carrie and Dave. "Whah," exclaimed Dave as he put his arms over his head.

Carrie held on to Harriet tighter, but she also focused the torch on the spot the splash had come from as it retreated behind them. "Come on, Dave, you aren't scared when it comes to facing the placktoids."

"The placktoids are the known unknown. It's the unknown unknowns I don't like," he replied from under his armpit.

In the patch of light from Carrie's torch, a dark, wet shape rose. It was long and smooth-skinned and didn't appear to have a head. Carrie couldn't decide if that was a bad thing or not. On the one hand, she wished it had *some* kind of head; on the other hand, she worried about just what kind of head it might have. The thing rose a couple of metres or so, reaching nearly to the ceiling of the tunnel, before falling into the water like massive black sausage into a cauldron of boiling water. Ripples came sliding along the river surface towards them. The sound of the creature hitting the liquid repeated.

"Tell me you didn't see anything," said Dave.

"I didn't see anything." Suddenly, the surface of the river was alive with life. "And I'm not seeing anything right now." Wriggling creatures like soft-bodied millipedes teemed among the waves. Carrie wondered if they were the prey of the headless thing, and if its appearance had driven them to the surface. Though as it didn't seem to have a mouth, how it ate them she couldn't guess. She recalled being dragged through the river in its current after they fell in. Had she passed through a shoal of the organisms, or alongside their nemesis? She shuddered. She hoped the predator—if that was what it was—wouldn't try to have a nibble of Harriet, or Dave, or her.

Dave had lowered his arms and was muttering to himself as he clutched his briefing tablet in one hand. Carrie leaned closer. With horror she realised he was saying the word Gavin had told them opened the gateway. "Don't say that," she exclaimed. "We aren't ready to go back yet."

"I'm just practicing everything but the last syllable. I don't want to forget in the heat of the moment. We might not get a second chance."

"Oh, fair enough." Carrie had completely forgotten what the word was, so she was happy for Dave to handle that job. She was glad to have him along. Though he was a bit of a wimp sometimes, he stepped up to the mark when needed and she could rely on him in a tight spot. She hoped she would one day learn to be as level-headed as her friend. Then she would be a really effective Liaison Officer.

Assuming they got out of this alive.

The wriggling things were becoming easier to see. More light than the beams cast by Carrie's torch was shining on them. She turned to face the direction they were travelling. Rays of sunlight shone from a split in the ceiling and were dancing on the river's ripples. It was difficult to tell how large the split was because she couldn't judge the distance, but it looked worryingly narrow.

She nudged Dave and pointed ahead. He put away his briefing device and gripped his bag tightly. Carrie did the same. Assuming the gap was large enough for them to fit through, it was in the ceiling, and Harriet would have to tilt upwards to go through it.

A massive plop sounded behind them. Carrie gave a small shriek. Had the headless thing decided to sample this interesting new source of food? She didn't dare turn round. She didn't want the last thing she saw to be the organ it used to catch and eat its prey.

The exit loomed larger and the light pouring through it became blindingly bright. Wafts of warm air blew over Carrie, scented with dust. Her bag across her chest, she leaned forward and grasped onto the sides of Harriet's shell for dear life as she felt the robot tilt and lift. Her angle was worryingly sharp. Just as Carrie began to slip backwards towards the dark underground river, Harriet was through the split in the ceiling and out into the baking air of the surface of the placktoid planet.

From behind came the sound of a final huge plop.

CHAPTER TWENTY-THREE – DESPERATE MEASURES

The light on the surface after hours in near darkness was almost painful. It took several minutes of squinting and blinking before Carrie could make out more than vague shapes around her. The suns were also unbearably hot once more, and she was soon soaked in sweat.

"Where now?" called Dave, raising his voice over the whistle of the hot wind.

Harriet's speed was easier to gauge now that Carrie could see the ground beneath them. The robot was travelling at a tremendous rate. "I don't think it's up to us to decide," answered Carrie. "Harriet's in a hurry to take us somewhere."

As her eyes grew accustomed to the light, Carrie peered ahead and to the sides. As before, the barren mountains ranged around them. These didn't look familiar, however, and she concluded that they must have travelled far from the mountain the High Commander had taken over in their journey along the river and to and from the underground sand bank. She wondered if Harriet was returning them to the High Commander's lair, and if she also understood how little time they had left before they had to open the gateway to the future.

She shifted in her awkward seat, her muscles cramped and aching. She looked forward to getting back to her flat and seeing Toodles and Rogue again. Even though Toodles was reticent about showing her affection for Carrie, she knew that, deep down, the cat adored her. And Rogue was always pleased to see her. Then Carrie remembered what Gavin had said: that when they returned, their and the placktoids' actions in the past might have altered the course of history; that they might not even recognise the world they returned to. Her heart ached. She feared losing the things dear to her even more than she feared the placktoids.

"Look," shouted Dave and pointed ahead. At a dizzying speed, a mountain approached. A familiar mountain. The mountain where they had been taken to the placktoid High Commander. Carrie had been right. Harriet understood, and she was taking them back there so they could destroy him.

But there was something strange about the mountain. Its slopes weren't drab and matte as the others were. They sparkled silver. At first Carrie wondered if large numbers of the silver robots had broken down and been ejected down its slopes, but the silver sparks that glimmered in the light of two suns were moving. The movement appeared sluggish due to the distance. In fact they must have been zooming up and down the slopes.

"What's going on?" Carrie called to her friend.

He had one hand over his brow as he peered ahead. "I think...I think the robots are fighting."

"What?" Carrie rummaged in her bag. Liaison Officers carried observation equipment though she'd never had call to use it before. She found what she was looking for. A folded pair of what looked like eyeglasses. She opened them up and looked through them, rocking back and almost falling from Harriet as the glasses brought the mountainside before them into extremely close, sharp focus. Robots were engaging in some kind of battle on the slopes. Some of them had weapons, and they were blasting others who seemed to have nothing to defend themselves with. The assaulted robots were instead trying to overwhelm their attackers by sheer force of numbers, and using their pincers and other tools to damage them if they managed to get up close.

"What's going on?" asked Dave as he followed Carrie's lead and took out his observation spectacles.

"The placktoids have armed the evil robots the High Commander created, and they're fighting with the good robots." An idea about why that should be so formed in Carrie's mind, and she studied the surrounding landscape for confirmation. Her suspicions were correct. The good robots were flooding out of nearby mountains to the one infected with placktoids from the future. "I think it's like what happened to us before. The robots detected you were a foreign body and ejected you from the mountain, and they tried to eject the placktoids. Now that the robots in the surrounding mountains have detected the foreign placktoids, they're trying to clean the mountain out. They're treating them like an infestation."

As she scanned the foothills of the mountain an inkling of another idea began to form but faded before it could take shape. The slopes were thick with the bodies of fallen robots. "This is awful, Dave. We have to get there and destroy the High Commander. The good robots are on an automatic response program. They can't think. They won't stop no matter how many of them are destroyed trying to clean out the mountain."

Dave slapped Harriet's shell. "Come on, Harriet, faster. We don't have much time."

The damaged robot seemed to be going as fast as she could, however, for she didn't speed up. But the mountain was quickly approaching. Carrie wondered how much time they had left. Half an hour? Or less? "Come on, Harriet."

Dave's lips were moving silently. Probably muttering the gateway-opening word beneath his breath, Carrie thought.

"You know," called Carrie, "I don't think Harriet had anything to do with the evolution of immortal, thinking, evil placktoids."

"You think they came from...?" Dave nodded ahead.

"I do. I think the evil influence came from the future. It's a time loop. Their mythology is wrong."

"And you think we can break the loop?" shouted Dave over the wind. "If we destroy the

High Commander and the evil robots, the placktoids might not develop their desire to tyrannise the galaxy? We might change the future?"

There was no time to answer. They were at the mountain. Harriet shot up the side and Carrie and Dave had to cling on to avoid tumbling out and falling to their deaths. A tunnel entrance appeared ahead and, before they knew it, they were inside.

Harriet had the element of surprise, but the evil robots weren't slow to catch on that she had invaded their domain. Carrie and Dave's weapons were in their hands already. Carrie faced forward while Dave turned to defend their rear. Robots appeared in front, and Carrie blasted them to pieces. Hot shrapnel embedded itself in the rocky tunnel walls. She heard Dave fire and realised that robots must be approaching from behind, too.

But the lozenge-shaped silver machines that had been turned to the dark side were the least of her worries. They lacked maneuverability and the weapons they had were simple. No, these facsimile, replacement robots were easy to take care of. It was the placktoids themselves she was worried about.

As if drawn by Carrie's thoughts, a paperclip and pen placktoid appeared. Carrie fired double-handed, scoring long lines across both. She knew from experience that sometimes a single hit wasn't enough. To put them out of commission she had to inflict damage across a large area.

Satisfyingly, the two placktoids split in half and hit the tunnel floor.

In a second they were over and past them. Harriet flew confidently and at great speed towards her destination. The fans in the tunnels sometimes barely had time to open before she was through them, and she outpaced the evil robots that followed.

"Go Harriet," yelled Carrie, and added a whoop.

But her elation turned to dread. They rounded a corner and entered the cavern dotted with holes where Carrie had searched for Dave earlier. On the far side ranged eight or nine placktoids of all kinds. "Turn around, Dave," Carrie exclaimed. "I'll need a hand with these." She was already firing, cutting a swathe through their ranks. But the placktoids returned fire, and Harriet nearly spilled the two humans out as she swerved to avoid being hit.

For a moment, Carrie and Dave could do little but cling on, but the second Harriet levelled out they were firing, their beams hitting the placktoids from below. Two tumbled into the abyss, followed by a third.

A blinding, searing pain in her shoulder cut through Carrie. She screamed, smelling the scent of her own burnt flesh. Before she was aware what was happening, Dave was suddenly crushed on top of her and the light dimmed. Harriet had closed the lid of her shell, squashing Carrie and Dave together. There was a hiss of melting metal, a scorching heat penetrating

Harriet's interior, and the world turned upright.

Harriet juddered, glided, then hit the ground. Inside her, Carrie and Dave were shocked through with vibrations as she slid along the floor. She hit a wall and her lid sprang open. The two humans were thrown clear and landed heavily.

Carrie's weapons were knocked from her hands, and the second that she stopped moving she scrambled to find them. Springing to her feet with a weapon in each hand she quickly took stock of the situation. Dave was a few metres away, also rising and scanning for his firepower. Harriet—or what was left of her, for she was little more than a twisted, broken, melted lump of metal—was motionless against the wall of the chamber.

Carrie spun on her heel, wondering where they were; what part of the mountain Harriet had brought them to after bursting through the placktoid ranks. Then she saw she had brought them to the epicentre. Before them was the High Commander. An evil robot it had just created was emerging from its centre. They had only a second before it would fire.

CHAPTER TWENTY-FOUR – THE FLOOD

The black, sleek lines of the High Commander looked out of place in the smooth-walled chamber. Like all the other placktoids from the future, and like Carrie and Dave, it had no place here. No wonder the caretakers of the mountains, the silver robots left by the Creators, wanted to evict them. For the nth time, Carrie wondered where the Creators had gone and why they had left behind their creations to fend for themselves down the centuries.

Then like a bolt from the blue everything fell into place. The semi-organic mountain interiors, the blue liquid like lifeblood, the fans to keep the air moving. Finally, it all made sense.

"Shoot the walls," cried Carrie.

"What? Why?" shouted Dave.

"There's no time to explain. Just do it." Carrie fired with both hands, scoring long arcs down the walls of the chamber, which fizzled and smoked. Dave did the same. The robot was nearly complete. There was just enough time for the two to fire again before the robot exited the centre of the placktoid High Commander. "Now," called Carrie, "run."

Laser pulses from the High Commander hit the wall they passed as they left the chamber. But they went from the frying pan into the fire. Ahead of them placktoids were approaching. "You take these and cover me," said Carrie as she turned and fired again into the chamber that housed the High Commander.

Cutting through the placktoid ranks with laser beams, Dave glanced at Carrie over his shoulder. "What are you doing?"

She raised her weapons and shot the tunnel over her head. The pain from her shoulder was forgotten as her adrenaline surged. The scent of the burning wall was overpowering. It was like melted plastic and barbecued meat. "I'm trying to get the mountain to react."

"Okay...you're what?"

"It's alive. They're all alive. I can't believe I was so stupid not to figure it out. The mountains are the Creators. They made the robots, then made them self-replicating."

Dave shot an approaching, massive staple remover right in its gaping jaws. The machine split in two, knocking a paperclip and hole punch flying. Dave mowed them down as they struggled to rise.

"Carrie, have you lost it? What are you talking about?"

"Look around you. This isn't rock. It's living material, with that blue liquid running through it like blood. The fans draw air through the mountain and keep it oxygenated. The robots function like…I don't know…something like antibodies, dealing with foreign material, and they keep the mountains functioning. It's been staring us in the face all along."

"Watch out," exclaimed Dave. The placktoids had stopped attacking on his side, but more had entered the other side of the chamber they had just left. Carrie turned her attention from destroying the tunnel walls to the approaching threat. She blew the top off a stapler that was speeding towards them on caterpillar tracks and sliced a paperclip in two. Its bottom half continued on, leaving the top half to clatter to the floor, before it fell too.

"Damage the walls, Dave," she shouted. "We need to start a massive immune response. Now."

He began shooting at the walls. "How much time have we got?"

That question had been worrying Carrie, too. But they couldn't waste a moment checking. The minute they stopped fending off the placktoids they would be dead. The result would be the same if her plan to get the mountain to react and eject the placktoids failed. She swallowed. *Come on,* she thought. *Can't you feel us? Do something.*

"It's no good," said Dave. "We have to open the gateway. It's the only chance we've got." He opened his bag.

Damn. Carrie poured laser beams from both weapons into the waves of placktoids speeding towards them. A grinding from behind told her that the evil mechanical aliens were reattempting to approach from Dave's side. But she couldn't cover both directions. "Dave!"

A shudder ran through the mountain, knocking both humans from their feet. Carrie's shots went wild, and the gateway device flew out of Dave's hand. "No," they shouted and scrabbled for the black box, getting in each others' way. As Carrie's fingertips touched the edge of the box, another shudder like an earthquake threw her to one side. The surrounding walls, scarred with Carrie's weapon fire, buckled and bent.

The placktoids were also struggling to function within the moving, wrenching interior of the mountain. They continued to fire at Carrie and Dave, but their shots went wild, hitting their fellows and the walls, which seemed to excite further spasms in the mountain.

Dave lunged and landed with an agonised thump on the top of the gateway device, grimacing as the corners dug into him. "I've got it," he gasped.

Carrie was cursing her decision to use the mountains to attack the placktoids. They should have taken their opportunity to get out of there while they could. She was sure that the deadline to return to the future had passed.

The mountain shuddered and juddered so violently it was impossible to do anything but cling on to the floor. It felt as if it were lifting from its roots and moving across the plain. Carrie hadn't had a clear idea of what the mountain might do in response to a sustained, damaging attack on the inside. She wondered what might come next, and whether she and Dave would survive it.

As suddenly as it had started, the shuddering stopped. Carrie and Dave looked at each other. The placktoids that still functioned began to grind, whirr and vibrate as they rose from the floor. "Good job that's over," said Dave. He lifted the gateway device to his lips, opened his mouth...and a great deluge of blue liquid burst out of the wall behind him and gushed over his head.

The vessels in the mountain walls had risen to the surface and were opening. The blue liquid was pouring out everywhere. Dave was drenched. He moved out of the immediate downpour and opened his mouth to speak again. But the liquid had reached his knees and was flowing with such a strong current it unbalanced him. He staggered and almost dropped the box.

"It's cleaning us out," said Carrie. "It's washing us and the placktoids out."

Dave and Carrie simultaneously slipped to the floor and the current began dragging them along.

"What'll we do?" called Dave as he was pulled farther down the tunnel. "We'll drown."

The answer bumped Carrie on the back of her head. Spitting out blue liquid, she turned to see Harriet, who had been lifted by the rushing solution and carried out of the chamber. There was no way Carrie would be able to climb inside her. Harriet's lid was closed and they were both being born along at too fast a rate. But Carrie dug her fingers into the edge of her lower shell, where it had been bent out of shape and didn't close flush with the lid.

Her Liaison Officer toolkit was dragging across her chest and neck, pulling her down. She let go of Harriet with one hand just long enough to pull out a weapon and stuff it down her jumpsuit, then pull the strap over her head and release the bag. It sank with the weight of all the devices it contained. Carrie hoped against hope that they wouldn't need them, even though she knew deep down that it was too late: they were stuck here forever.

Harriet's buoyancy meant she travelled faster on the current than Dave, who was struggling to keep his head free of the liquid. Carrie and Harriet quickly caught up with him.

"Grab on," called Carrie as Harriet's front end nudged Dave's sinking figure.

His knuckles were white where he gripped the gateway device in one hand. The other hand he slotted into a gap between Harriet's upper and lower shell. His Liaison Officer bag was also missing, lost in the flood.

Bits and pieces of placktoid tumbled through the liquid as it rose higher in the tunnel, flowing with the two humans as they were born downwards and out of the mountain. Would they reach the outside before the liquid rose to the tunnel roof and drowned them?

Being made of metal, the placktoids were being washed out of the mountain more slowly than the humans, it seemed. At least, no whole placktoid threatened them as they were carried along, which was just as well because, as Carrie realised, with both hands occupied with saving their lives, they couldn't defend themselves.

Harriet, Carrie and Dave crashed into an awkward corner and spun twice in a vortex before they were torn free. Dave disappeared below the surface for a worryingly long time. All Carrie could see of him was the one hand with bloody knuckles gripping Harriet's shell, and the other hand holding the gateway device aloft. As his head finally broke free, he gave a great gasp.

Carrie was so preoccupied with her friend's plight that she didn't notice they were rapidly approaching the tunnel entrance until it was too late. Before they could do anything to prevent it —not that there was anything they could have done—she, Dave and Harriet were flying through the air, born out of the mountain and down the side on a clear blue wave.

CHAPTER TWENTY-FIVE – PAINFUL PARTING

When the blue liquid had mixed with the fine dust of the desert and created a sludge, and Carrie had tumbled to a stop, she crawled across the wet sand to reach her friend. The waterfall had borne them careening down and deposited them at the mountain's base. Dave was only a short distance away, caked in the thin mud. He was lying on his back, holding the gateway device aloft and tossing restlessly from side to side.

"What's wrong?" she asked. "Are you hurt?"

"I can't remember. I can't remember," he exclaimed.

"You...?" Carrie wondered if he'd hit his head before she understood what he meant. He couldn't remember the word to activate the device. Her heart rose into her throat. But surely they were out of time anyway? "We still have a job to do. We have to destroy the High Commander so he stops creating the evil robots."

"There's no time. We have to leave now. We have to get back." Dave's eyes were wild. Perhaps he had hit his head after all. "What was it? Chagganooga? Chumbawumba?

Crispynoodle?"

"Dave," Carrie said gently, "I think—"

A rumble like thunder sounded from above. Was it finally going to rain on the arid planet? She looked up, but there were no clouds. Instead, she noticed that, as well as liquid flowing from all the tunnel exits on the mountain, it was also leaking from a solid patch on the side.

Dave thumped his head in frustration, but Carrie watched the patch, her head tilted. Rocks were breaking loose and sliding down on the newly created stream of blue liquid. She rubbed her eyes. She could swear that the mountainside was bulging, as if something were pushing out from within.

"Dave," she said. Her friend didn't reply. "Dave."

"What?" he spat.

Carrie silently pointed upwards. If she was right, and something was behind that patch of mountain, about to be ejected, they were right under where it would land.

"Oh, great," said Dave. "That's all we need."

They both leaped up and sped away, Dave still clutching the gateway device. Another rumble came from behind, followed by an explosion that ripped through the air. "To the side," shouted Carrie, "to the side." If they were in the thing's trajectory it made no sense to keep running forward. They veered to the right. Carrie's legs ached and her lungs heaved. The wound on her shoulder nagged. She was reaching the end of her strength, and Dave was staggering with exhaustion.

A massive boom from the ground behind them and a vibration in the sand told Carrie the mountain had ejected something very large and very solid. She had a good idea of what it might be: the largest foreign body that had been infecting the mountain and creating malignant versions of its own beneficial organisms. A low flood of liquid washed across their feet. Carrie risked a look over her shoulder. "Stop, it's okay."

The placktoid High Commander lay at a crazy angle at the foot of the mountain. The liquid that had borne it out was draining away. Above, there was a large hole in the mountainside. The liquid flowing from it was diminishing at a rapid rate. The mountain had rid itself of its interloper at last.

The placktoid High Commander was battered and broken, but Carrie was taking no chances. This would be her only opportunity to put an end to it for once and for all and prevent it from making any more of the evil robots. She began to run towards it, drawing out the weapon she had stuffed down her jumpsuit.

"Carrie," called Dave. "I remember. I can remember the word. Leave it."

"It's too late now anyway," she called back. "We're too late. I'm sorry."

"No, I thought of something."

But Carrie took no more notice. She was within firing range of the High Commander. A laser pulse flew from it, narrowly missing her. It was still alive. And it wanted her dead. Carrie blasted it, searing through its central base, slicing through its walls. The placktoid returned fire with its dying power, catching Carrie's thigh. She screamed and fell in agony. Her weapon flew from her grasp. This was it. She was defenceless, and the High Commander was going to kill her with its last dregs of energy.

But laser pulses appeared from behind and passed over her head to hit the placktoid square in its middle. The thing blew apart, and black metal shards thunked to the dust.

Dave collapsed breathless beside Carrie in the wet dust. They had done it. They had completed their mission, or at least they had done the best they could.

"I thought you were opening the gateway," Carrie said, trying to block the pain from her leg and shoulder.

"Yeah, and leave you to die?"

She rubbed her eyes, which were leaking. "I'm sorry."

"For what?"

"For making us late. We've missed our chance, haven't we? They've put the time shield down. We can't get out."

"Maybe, and maybe not." Dave held up the gateway device. It was covered in mud but whole and unmarked. He had clearly protected it with his life as they were tossed around and ejected from the mountain. "The gateway engineers got their calculations wrong when they sent us. What if they got them wrong when they laid down the time shield?"

"You mean they could have put it down ages ago, or maybe...?"

"Maybe not yet."

Carrie's eyes widened. "We could still have a chance." She paused and frowned. "But what happens if the time shield is already there when we try to pass through the gateway? What'll happen to us? Gavin didn't say."

"Whatever happens, could it be worse than staying here?" They both surveyed the barren, inhospitable place. Carrie shook her head.

"Right, let's try, okay?"

Carrie looked into her friend's eyes. "Okay."

Dave held up the device and said, "Chacknolokankle."

If the time shield was down and their passage to the future was blocked, the familiar green spiral might not appear, but a mist formed and began to solidify and spin.

"It's working so far," Dave said hopefully.

Carrie chose not to remind him of what Gavin had warned them, that even if they did manage to get back to their own time their world might be so altered as to be unrecognisable. If that was the case, assuming they didn't disappear into the ether, at least they would have each other, Carrie thought.

Dave placed the box on the ground. "You

first." Carrie took a final look around. Her heart fell. A short distance away lay a familiar broken, busted silver robot. At first glance the machine might have been indistinguishable from all the others, but Carrie knew every dent, every twist and every graze of the silver shell by heart. It was Harriet. The friend who had saved their lives innumerable times. And Carrie had nearly forgotten her. She began to run.

"Carrie," shouted Dave.

"You go first," she called back.

"No."

"I have to speak to Harriet. Please, go. I'll be right behind you."

She skidded to a stop next to the stricken robot. Was she even still alive? Carrie put a hand on the mangled shell where drops of blue liquid still lingered, rapidly evaporating under the heat of the two suns. "You're coming with me." She began to drag Harriet towards the gateway.

Barely audible above the sound of her shell scraping along the ground, Harriet made a noise. It sounded like, "No."

Carrie's hands fell away. She couldn't believe her ears. "Harriet, did you speak? Can you speak?"

"I learn."

"Harriet, you're alive. This is wonderful. You can come with us." She looked over her shoulder to see Dave hesitating before the swirling gateway. "Go, please," she called.

"Not without you," he called back. She returned her attention to Harriet.

"No. I stay," said the robot. "I help my people."

CHAPTER TWENTY-SIX – BORROWED TIME

It was a weeping Carrie who crashed into Dave in the gateway room of the Transgalactic Council starship. Several minutes passed before he could get any sense out of her. When her sobs finally subsided and she had rubbed her eyes with her knuckles and wiped her nose on her sleeve, she explained what Harriet had said, and that she hadn't had time to persuade the robot to come with her through the gateway.

Dave sat silent for a moment before saying gently, "She was probably right, Carrie. She belongs back there in the placktoid past, helping to undo the damage the placktoids from the future caused."

Carrie sniffed. "I know. I know you're right. I just...I just wanted more time with her, you know? After all she'd done for us, after all we'd been through together, I wanted to get to know her. But we only had seconds before the gateway would fade to nothing. And I had to choose. I had to choose between staying there and helping Harriet, and coming back here to you, and Gavin, and my family and friends, and Earth, and even my stupid call centre job...oh." Her face fell. "Well, not that anyway, but..." Her eyes were leaking again.

Dave rested a hand on her arm. "You couldn't have done much to help Harriet. You wouldn't have lasted more than a few days."

"But she was all alone there, Dave. All she had were the other robots who couldn't think and the evil placktoids. Imagine it. It would be like being the last person left alive, only worse. All around would be people who looked human but couldn't communicate with you, and other humans who were out to get you. How long will Harriet last in a situation like that?"

"If she had no fixed life span like the myth said, she could live a long time. And she could repair herself, or maybe she could override another robot's programming and make it repair her."

"She won't live that long," said Carrie, shaking her head. "I left her out on the plain. The placktoids or the evil robots will find her and finish her off."

"I don't see how. She looks like any other robot. How would they know it was her? They identified her before by what she was doing, not how she looked. The placktoids knew her behaviour was out of the ordinary. That was why they targeted her. And she's smart enough to know that. As long as she copies the behaviour of the other robots while she's around the placktoids, she should be safe. And we destroyed the High Commander, don't forget."

Carrie's tense expression relaxed a little. "Maybe you're right. I hope so."

The two stood and for the first time realised they were alone in the gateway room. Dave put his hands on his hips. "Not much of a welcoming committee."

Carrie felt nearly dead with exhaustion. She was covered head to toe in grainy mud, which seemed to have worked its way into every nook and cranny. Her muscles ached with tiredness, the burns from the placktoid weapons throbbed, and she felt emotionally wrung out to dry. She didn't want a welcoming committee. All she wanted was to see her pets, have a warm bath and get into a soft bed. But it was strange. Where was Gavin? Where were Errruorerrrrrhch and all the other Council Managers who had been so admiring of the fact them when they left?

Dave was staring at her, his mouth open to an O.

"What? What are you thinking?" Carrie asked.

"Don't you remember what they said? By changing something in the past, we could affect the course of history and return to a different present."

Carrie's hands flew to her face. "Oh no," she said between her fingers. "You mean Gavin might not exist? Or the Council?" She frowned. "But that can't be right. We're on the Council starship. Or, at least, everything looks the same, don't you think?"

"Yeah, but where is everyone?"

Carrie and Dave left the gateway room with

its now-blank screen and set off down the creamy ceramic corridors of the Council vessel. The environment reminded Carrie strongly of the tunnels in the placktoid mountains...or, rather, the tunnels within the Creators, she reminded herself. Though the starship was almost uncomfortably warm, she shivered. It would be a long time before she felt comfortable in confined spaces again.

They passed recesses set into the sides, floors and ceilings of the corridors, surrounded by weird symbols. From time spent training on a Council starship, Carrie knew the panels would only open to pheromones excreted by Council managers, or DNA signatures programmed into them. She tried placing her hand on a few of the doors but met with a predictable lack of success.

"What are we going to do if we can't find anyone?" asked Dave. "We don't know how to open a gateway to Earth. How will we get home?"

Carrie was wondering the same thing as a terrible smell hit her. "Oh, wow," she said, and covered her nose and mouth with a hand. The reek was a mixture of rotting fish, paint thinner and a vicious case of salmonella poisoning. Her eyes watered, and she clamped her teeth together to fight an urge to vomit. "I think the managers might be this way," she said in a nasal whine, gripping her nose between thumb and forefinger.

Both turning a sickly shade of pale green, Carrie and Dave reluctantly followed the stench where it led them. The managers weren't far away, but they'd been hard to detect because they were making no sound. The two humans stumbled into a room packed with the massive insectoid aliens that the Council employed as its managers. They were standing still and communicating through their species' traditional method: the excretion of pheromones.

Nearly all the managers were ranged around three-quarters of the room and facing in one direction. In the corner of the room was a pool shot through with light that coruscated, glimmered and flashed. A single manager was draped over the pool, suspended by the claws of its ten pairs of legs, which were only just wide enough to prevent it from falling in. To Carrie and Dave, the scene was frozen, though the odour in the room implied a heated debate was going on.

So intent were the managers on their discussion, it took a moment or two for any of them to notice the humans' arrival. The manager that spotted them skittered sideways in surprise and collided with another. Within a few moments the room was in motion, though the communications were still meaningless to Carrie and Dave because the insectoid aliens continued to use their pheromone language.

A single voice sounded across the room. "Carrie and Dave. It is most pleasant to see you have arrived back safely." The voice seemed to come from the manager suspended over the pool.

"Gavin?" said Carrie.

"Yes, it is I. I imagine it must be difficult for you to tell one manager from another. I have a similar problem with humans and other species, but I have the advantage of—"

"What are you doing? Why on Earth are you hanging over that water?"

"You are mistaken. The liquid beneath me is not hydrogen dioxide. This is the transgalactic gateway control centre. You see...ah..." He paused. "I am afraid that English does not yet contain the words to explain its contents or operation."

Carrie was marching through the ranks of managers to Gavin's side. He looked in need of some help. As she reached him, however, he said, "Please do not approach me, Carrie. I have achieved a state of perfect balance. One touch and I would probably fall in."

"And then what would happen?"

"Ah...by most accounts, an excruciating death would ensue."

Carrie stepped back. Another Council manager joined them. "He has been exceedingly foolish."

"Errruorerrrrrh?"

The manager chittered. "Errruorerrrrrhch," she said, with special emphasis on the 'ch'. "I do not know how we will get him off there now. I hope he does not die while we are determining the method that is the safest and most likely to succeed."

"I hope so too," exclaimed Carrie. "But what's going on? Gavin, what are you doing hanging over the transgalactic gateway control?"

When Gavin didn't reply, Errruorerrrrrhch answered for him. "When the deadline for applying the time shield arrived, he threw himself across the control centre to block the engineers' access. He stated that he would not move until you and Dave had returned. We could not do anything. The engineers could not approach the centre, and we could not move Gavin without risking that he fall into the centre and destroy it, thereby further preventing the engineers from applying the time shield."

Errruorerrrrrhch continued speaking, but Carrie couldn't make out what the alien was saying. She was crying again.

CHAPTER TWENTY-SEVEN – FAREWELL TO GAVIN

The Transgalactic Council wanted Carrie and Dave to stay longer than the several hours it took to heal their wounds and debrief them on their assignment, but both wanted nothing more than to go home. They had told the managers everything that had happened and how the mountains that everyone had assumed were part of the placktoid planet's geology were actually the placktoid's Creators. That information had caused quite a stir. They had apparently solved one of the great mysteries of the galaxy.

But Carrie couldn't relax and enjoy her success. She missed her pets, and though she knew the Council engineers would return her to the time just a few minutes after she had originally left—a small time hop they could complete accurately—she couldn't wait for Rogue to jump up and slobber over her face in the habit she had been trying to train him out of for several years.

For a standard transgalactic gateway journey, they could leave from anywhere on the ship. They chose a small, quiet room that looked out over the local star field. The patterns were completely unfamiliar to Carrie, but she assumed that they, like everything else she and Dave had experienced so far, were unchanged from the galaxy they had left when they journeyed into the past. The thought comforted her now that she was about to return home. She didn't want to think that anything might be different. She liked her life just as it was, though now she had to find a new job.

"I am afraid I must say goodbye for the foreseeable future," said Gavin.

"What?" exclaimed Carrie. "Why? Have I been transferred to another manager?"

"No, that is not the reason it may be some time before we can meet again. I have been dismissed from my role at the Transgalactic Council. As this is my third dismissal, I am permanently banned from applying for any further positions."

"Oh no," said Carrie. "Was it because of what you did for us? That's so unfair."

"Sorry to hear that, mate," said Dave.

"Can't you appeal? You saved our lives. Isn't a manager supposed to look after his staff?"

"I cannot appeal, but I would not do so in any case. The Council is perfectly correct to dismiss me. I jeopardised the fate of the galaxy for the sake of two members of staff. It was unconscionable. And yet at the time it seemed to be the correct thing to do.

"I am going to reflect on my behaviour and try to understand the underlying philosophical implications while I am seeking further employment."

"Won't I ever see you again?" Tears were welling up in Carrie's eyes. She felt like she'd done enough crying over the last few hours to last her a lifetime.

"We may certainly meet if you ever come to my home planet, or perhaps our paths will cross elsewhere, or if Earth joins the Unity, I shall pay you and Dave a visit."

Carrie imagined the stir Gavin would create walking through Northampton town centre. "I'm definitely going to come and see you as soon as I get a chance."

"Have there been any reports of the placktoids yet?" asked Dave.

"Nothing as yet. As far as we can tell at the moment, your assignment was successful. It appears no placktoids left the planet before the time shield finally went up. By hiding in the past and trying to change the course of history, the placktoids sealed their own fate. They seem to be trapped."

Carrie was tempted to reopen a discussion she'd had with Gavin about the nature of time, and whether it was possible that the placktoids were the engineers of their own path to evil, but Gavin's responses had made her head spin. All she had understood was the 'we don't know' part. She decided to leave it at that.

"All ready?" asked Dave.

Carrie nodded and gingerly wrapped her arms around Gavin's massive bronze head, with its compound eyes and double, razor-sharp mandibles. It was an awkward hug, but she wouldn't feel right without giving him one.

The familiar green mist appeared from nowhere in front of the star field that occupied one wall of the room. Though Carrie's heart rose at the prospect of going home, the feeling was bittersweet knowing she wouldn't see Gavin for a while, perhaps forever. She'd grown accustomed to his terrifying appearance and now she couldn't see him as anything other than an old, very dear friend; a friend to whom she owed her life.

Dave approached the insectoid alien with his hand outstretched but balked when Gavin raised a claw to shake it. He gingerly grasped one of Gavin's antennae and waggled it instead.

Carrie took a final look at the glittering expanse that lay outside the ship. She stepped forward. The air rushing towards the gateway lifted her and pulled her in, then she was home.

CHAPTER TWENTY-EIGHT – TRANSMOGRIFIED MOGGIE

At first, Carrie thought the Council gateway engineers had sent her through to the wrong place. She didn't recognise the kitchen floor she slid across as she arrived back on Earth. When Dave's boots appeared through the green mist, she scrambled out of his way and stood up. Turning on her heel, she took in the large room filled with the latest domestic appliances. Fear gripped her heart, but it was quickly dispelled when Rogue bounded in and leapt up to lick her face.

So she *was* home, but her home was quite different from the poky little flat she remembered.

"Woah," said Dave. "It looks like we did change something."

"But how?" asked Carrie. "How could something we did thousands of years ago on a planet millions of light years away have given me a posh house?" She looked out the window and found she recognised the street. Her former flat was in the building opposite. She was back in

Northampton, and in nearly the same spot, but not quite.

"Beats me," said Dave. "But don't look a gift horse in the mouth. Anyway, I'm shattered. I'm going home. Maybe I'll have moved to a mansion. See you later." Grabbing his jacket from the back of the kitchen chair, he left.

Carrie explored her new home. First of all she looked for Toodles, and found her fast asleep on a bookshelf. As she investigated further, she realised her new home was the most upmarket house she'd ever lived in, including the place where she grew up. She was relieved to find she seemed to live alone. An unfamiliar boyfriend or husband would have been very difficult to deal with.

After the long, hot bath she'd promised herself, she settled down to sleep. Tomorrow she would have to start job-hunting. Maybe she had a mortgage to pay on the house? Carrie yawned. She was too tired to think about it. She would have to find out in the morning.

Her phone rang. She reached and grabbed it from the polished wooden bedside table. It was Dave. "Hi, are you calling from your mansion?"

"No, I'm back in the same old place, worst luck. How about you? Are you enjoying your life of luxury?"

"I'm enjoying it while I can. For all I know I could be up to my eyeballs in debt. I'm going to start looking on job websites in the morning."

"I don't think you'll need to do that."

"Why? Even if I own this place I've got to eat."

"Carrie, when I got home I checked my payslips to make sure I still had the same job. I thought it would be embarrassing to turn up somewhere that no one had heard of me. And...well...are you sitting down?"

"I'm lying down, Dave. I'm really tired. Whatever it is you want to tell me, spit it out."

"Well...apparently I work for Carrie Hatchett Enterprises."

Carrie sat bolt upright, her exhaustion banished. "What?" she squeaked.

"It looks like you own the company, call centre and everything. It's all yours."

"What?"

"I said you—"

"I heard you, but, I mean, how?"

"Who knows? It's good news, though, isn't it? You won't have to find another job."

"I suppose so." Carrie's mind was reeling. How on Earth could she run a company?

"Anyway, we can talk tomorrow. I can barely keep my eyes open. I've got another reason for phoning you. The weather forecast says it's going to be freezing, and the bus is always late when it's like that. I don't suppose you could give me a lift to work?"

"But I don't have a...have I got a car?"

"It's parked right in your driveway. Didn't you notice?"

"I didn't think to look. Cool. Yeah, of course. I'll pick you up about eight."

Carrie turned her phone to silent and put it on the table next to her bed. She owned a company? It sounded a little scary, but this new life seemed to be getting better and better. She lay down, turned on her side and tucked her arm under her pillow. Just as she was about to close her eyes, she saw movement at her bedroom door, which she had left ajar. Ginger movement.

She was suddenly very awake. Was Toodles mounting a nighttime attack? She didn't usually launch an offensive unprovoked. Maybe the cat had remembered Carrie and Dave's rude attempt to remove her from the kettle and she was seeking revenge?

A ball of fur landed on the bed. Toodles' amber eyes surveyed the stock-still Carrie, who had learned through painful experience that motion was perceived in a negative light by her cat. An unfamiliar, low buzz sounded in Carrie's ears. Could it be? Was it possible? Was Toodles *purring*?

The cat rubbed her face against Carrie's. This *was* Toodles, right? Carrie held her breath. Very slowly, she pulled a hand from beneath the covers and, very tentatively, stroked her pet. Toodles responded by curling into a ball next to Carrie's head, her soft fur tickling her nose.

"Toodles," breathed Carrie, "what's happened to you?"

She could get very used to this new life. Very used to it indeed. She finally slid into a deep, furry sleep.

CARRIE'S STORY CONTINUES IN...

CARRIE'S CALAMITY

Sign up to my reader group for a free copy of *Carrie Hatchett's Christmas*, the standalone novelette in the Carrie Hatchett, Space Adventurer series, and for exclusive notice of new releases, advanced reader opportunities and other interesting stuff:

https://jjgreenauthor.com/free-books/

ALSO BY J.J. GREEN

STAR MAGE SAGA

SPACE COLONY ONE

SHADOWS OF THE VOID

LOST TO TOMORROW

THERE COMES A TIME
A SCIENCE FICTION COLLECTION

DAWN FALCON
A FANTASY COLLECTION